**PURE
SLUSH
BOOKS**

A
CLUSTER
OF
LIGHTS

A
CLUSTER
OF
LIGHTS

Then and now:
52 writers
around the world

an anthology

edited by

Michelle Elvy

and

John Wentworth Chapin

First published as a collection May 2023
Content copyright © Pure Slush Books and individual authors
Edited by Michelle Elvy and John Wentworth Chapin
Formatted and designed by Matt Potter

ISBN: 978-1-923000-00-1

BP#00116

Pure Slush Books
32 Meredith Street
Sefton Park SA 5083
Australia

Email: edpureslush@live.com.au
Website: pureslush.com
Store: pureslush.com/store

Cover design copyright © Matt Potter
Original cover image copyright © kytalpa

Also available as an ePub eBook
ISBN: 978-1-923000-10-0
Also available as a Kindle eBook
ISBN: 978-1-923000-03-2

A note on differences in punctuation and spelling
Pure Slush Books proudly features writers from across the English-speaking world.
Some speak and write English as their first language, while for others, it's their second
or third or even fourth language. Naturally, across all versions of English, there are
differences in punctuation and spelling, and even in meaning. These differences are
reflected in the work *Pure Slush Books* publishes, and they account for any differences
in punctuation, spelling and meaning found within these pages.

Pure Slush Books is a member of the
Bequem Publishing collective
bequempublishing.com/

FEATURING THE WRITING OF

Alex Reece ABBOTT • Tina BARRY • Chelsea BIONDOLILLO

Walter BJORKMAN • Marty BRICK • Diane BROWN

John Wentworth CHAPIN • James CLAFFEY

Sheldon Lee COMPTON • Bob ECKSTEIN

David EGGLETON • KM ELKES • Lola ELVY

Michelle ELVY • Nod GHOSH • Kelly GROTKE

Jane HAMMONS • Stephen HASTINGS-KING

Mary Jane HOLMES • Randal HOULE • Gail INGRAM

Abha IYENGAR • Lynn JENNER • Erik KENNEDY • Jen KNOX

Len KUNTZ • Nathan Alling LONG • S J MANNION

Al McDERMID • Michelle McEWEN • Catherine McNAMARA

Anna NAZAROVA-EVANS • Piet NIEUWLAND

James NORCLIFFE • Tom O'BRIEN • Nuala O'CONNOR

Michael PARKER • Gary PERCESEPE • Stella PIERIDES

Meg POKRASS • Darryl PRICE • Sam RASNAKE

John RILEY • Robert SCOTELLARO • Rachel SMITH

Maggie SOKOLIK • Andrew STANCEK • T M UPCHURCH

Robert VAUGHAN • Linda WASTILA • Derek Ivan WEBSTER

Iona WINTER • Cherise WOLAS

INTRODUCTION

This project was born from a year of intense creativity in 2010/11. The goal was to work week by week to hone our skills and develop our writing practice. When we started *52/250 – A Year of Flash*, we had no idea what would come. A year of writing, a year of friendships. But it was the beginning of something for many of us: more years of writing, and writing better; more years of friendships.

For this new anthology, we read many excellent stories, from familiar 52|250 writers and also newcomers. We are grateful to everyone who submitted—and of course to everyone who took part in *52/250 – A Year of Flash!*

The result is in your hands. A multinational collection of 52 writers, including 34 from the 2010/11 project, each conjuring a response to a small piece written in an earlier time. Writers from across the globe come together ten years later to celebrate the small story, 250 words at a time.

Special thanks to Matt Potter, whose involvement as one of the original 52|250 writers led to him establishing a publishing house in 2010 in his home city of Adelaide. It's fitting that, a decade later, we're collaborating to publish this book.

We dedicate this anthology to the memory of our co-editor Walter Bjorkman. Walt lived and wrote with his own inimitable style and energetically contributed to this community. His voice is here, too, with the first and last of the pieces he wrote for 52|250; they close this volume.

Michelle Elvy & John Wentworth Chapin
Dunedin & Baltimore, May 2023

CONTENTS

MAPS

Sheldon Lee Compton
A Mountain So Lost (2010)

Maps are everywhere. On the palm of your hand, across the terrain of your heart. These are maps of hope and magic, emotion and muscle.

But these are not real maps, not those of a draftsman. Not the cartographic maps I make, the general progression from the cave wall to my fingers. The others, the tracks and cuts left on the heart, the spill of superstition poured over the heads of the desperate. These maps are not science. They have no more direction to offer than a wind-beaten cloud.

They call what I did a deliberate error, cartographic graffiti. I like that. It's better than saying it was a prank or joke. It paints me less like a clown and more as a mischievous eccentric. Being different and clever is how I will be remembered.

In my design for the Rocky Mountains' continental divide I added a fictitious peak called Mount Richard. It took two years before anyone realized there was no such peak, no mountain bearing my namesake. Two years I spent pointing out me, the mountain, to Heather in the diner in Niwot, to Jill at a bar in Arvada, Kim in Broomfield, Teresa in Wheat Ridge, at least four dozen or more across Colorado.

I should have just kept quiet, stood in silence against the skyline and let the majesty do the talking. I should have learned to be patient in my loneliness, still enough to watch a rosebud bloom.

First published in 52|250 – A Year of Flash

Sheldon Lee Compton
A Common Creation (2020)

It didn't all begin with a mapping of the earth. The first maps are in no way science. It didn't all begin with mountains or rocks. It began before that. It began in the air. In the air all around everything. What they later called the cosmos. The galaxy. The universe. So many names for nothing that becomes something.

The map maker would say that order is truth, the sectioning and positioning of what we have, of what we can see, is mapped as a supreme honesty. And that the air is the air and should be named nothing, as it offers no more beauty to what can be marked and measured off for all history.

But then a rosebud coming to bloom is prime beauty. The slow movement of the petals up through the mist is a slow explosion yawning. Neither can be transformed into lines and legends and bar scales. A compass rose can give the ship its direction but not its purpose.

This exploding, though divine, isn't rare. It's how everything is everything. Creation, even the first creation, is never the only force moving through the centillions of days and nights that make up the time we have. Nothing turns into something all the time.

Linda Wastila
It's true what they say (2011)

…and when I open my eyes I see what a perfect shot, the arrow stuck in the side of my neck, a fountain of blood sinking the snow like maple sap, and Dave barrels through underbrush, his breath heaves white clouds, he's lost his hat, there's a bald spot in back I'd never noticed because even though he's my little brother he's five inches taller, and he sinks to his knees, shit, shit, shit, oh shit, then fumbles in his camo for his cell and I laugh, you idiot, you fucking know you can't get a signal this side of the mountain, but he jabs at the stupid buttons anyway, and then Pa grasps my fingers, odd because he's never held my hand and he's dead ten years anyway, and he says with his eyes, it's time to go, and below spins green and white, this brilliant heat fills me, and I turn to Pa and say, hey it's true what they say on those tv shows, those people who die and come back, and when he smiles I know I'm dead and it's okay this peace falls over me, a kind of grace I feel after I mow the hayfield all sweaty and happy, and when I think of Marisa, the swell of her belly, and I wait for the tug, the one that yanks me back to Dave blubbering over me in the cold bloody snow, I wait and wait, but Pa grips me harder and…

First published in 52 | 250 – A Year of Flash

Linda Wastila
Second Shift
in the Cannery (2021)

After a while the fish look the same, smell the same, taste the same. We rest the same spiny sardines in the same squat tin cans ribboned in blue and yellow plastic. Perched on the same stolid stools, our trunks thick from lard and white bread, we look the same in our hairnets, our green rubberized aprons, blue masks, and pink latex gloves. When the three o'clock wails we smell the same, and if you licked our foreheads they'd taste the same. It's the smell that gives us away, the briny oily smell of fish innards, a smell that no amount of showering or deodorant covers, and when we mingle with the other women in town in the grocery aisles and church pews and widow support groups, you can smell who works at the cannery and who works at the meat processing plant (pay is higher at the meat factory but we widows don't do meat, can't do anything with blood). In our cars, we adjust our lipsticks—pink, red, coral—and spray our perfumes, and the lucky ones drive home and settle in the arms of the ones they love and who love them, and we unlucky ones order out from the Chinese place on Main Street, always vegetarian, and we become ourselves.

Jen Knox
Wave (2010)

The thing about a corner like this is that it doesn't matter what city it's in. It's that corner from which you stand and see only bars, a convenience store, and a series of signs that promise if you buy two of something—boxes of cigarettes, bags of potato chips, two-liter bottles of soda—you get the third free.

The thing about a corner like this is that if you drive by, or you're stopped at the light and you glance out your car window, you can only think about the light turning green and where you need to be because that place is suddenly waiting for you. Because the thing about a corner like this is that it's not going anywhere. It's too common, too anonymous to loom.

And if you live on a corner like this, at the core, you are too common, too anonymous to matter. So, if you live on a corner like this, like we do, wave at the people who drive by, smile at them, and take heart when they look surprised.

First published in 52 | 250 – A Year of Flash

Jen Knox
Wave (2021)

There is nothing common here now. We adopt labels and sub-labels, fitting out to fit in, terrified of being clustered into a group of unfortunate norms. We used to wave from street corners, and now we stare out windows. Those who drive by are our neighbors, essential, angels. Maybe we are, too.

There is an app for sky-watching, and we use it to speak to the moon. We see the stars and planets so much clearer as the neighborhood remains without light pollution or synthetic sound. We try to listen to the stars as we stand near a store that's barely hanging on, weighed down by news yet twirling beneath possibility as liquor tastes less interesting than the future.

We imagine our former selves dipping into the present day and being horrified. But then we laugh. Because we can laugh. Because we're moving forward. When we wave from street corners, we wave at the sky. There's no need to wave at each other because we're all here together, ready to take another step.

Andrew Stancek
Mirko's Mountain (2011)

Mirko waits for his father to catch up. The climb is steep; the afternoon sun is baking.

"Time for us to get out of this hellish city," Father said in the morning, surveying the wreckage of the apartment. "Mountains, real air, shepherds, *zincica*. I'll take you to Rosutec; show you where I proposed to your mother." Mirko snorted. Many promises under the bridge, many lofty plans. By nightfall Father was sure to be drinking with Janka or Dasenka or Lesia somewhere.

"Can you give me some grocery money?" he asked. Father opened the fridge, saw the yawning emptiness.

"You wishing you were back with your mother? Roast pork, dumpling, sauerkraut?"

"Hell, no," Mirko laughed. "More excitement. But can I have money anyway?"

Father roared, "Chip off the old block," handing him a hundred-crown note.

But before noon they are on the train to Zilina and now are climbing. Mirko looks back. In the city Father stops at every street corner to catch his breath; here his face is flushed but his step has spring.

When Father steps over the last boulder, they admire the vista. The meadow is flecked with grazing sheep. Wood smoke rises out of a shepherd hut, rock crags, tree-covered hillsides, rising mist. A village no more than a speck lies below them.

"All these things I will give you, if you fall down and worship me," Father turns to him.

Mirko kicks a stone, laughing. "I'll take it; I'll take it."

First published in 52|250 – A Year of Flash

Andrew Stancek
Mirko's Mountain Yet Again (2022)

Mirko huffs as they climb the last ascent and suddenly they're at the top and he's breathing in the freezing air and hints of gladness, startled anew by the view from Rosutec Mountain.

Vierka stomps her feet, first time here, not sure yet whether this prematurely grey man with the outline of a paunch is worth the effort.

"It *is* gorgeous," she says. "No word of a lie there." He reaches out and wraps her in a bear hug.

A flock of sheep grazes far below, bells tinkle, a hawk soars.

"Father proposed to Mother here," Mirko says. "Years later, when I was scrambling for a new start, he and I climbed up and then lived together for a while. I buried him after about two years, but we cooked some mean stews together, swallowed our hurts."

They breathe in silence for a while.

Mirko kneels. "It's pretty quick, I know, but I think we're a good fit. I'll try to make you happy, I will. Will you?" He's presenting a ring, his eyes lit up.

She squints into the sun, opens her mouth – no sound comes out. She brushes her hair back, rips off a hairband, sends it twirling towards the firs.

Mirko zips the ring into a pocket, glowering. "We can take more time if you want, if you're not certain."

She bolts like a mountain goat, stumbles on a rock, slides but does not slow down, does not look back.

Meg Pokrass

There is Only So Much Liquid (2011)

A few nights ago, on her fortieth birthday, Janelle was drunk from absinthe at the Beachside bar, lit like an oil lamp from within—ready to hit the water in the dark and swim for it before another birthday. Who would know?

Two men were kissing sweetly and playfully by the door. Her eyes felt stuck. She wanted to say something—to ask if she could join.

Today at the ocean the sun feels half-cocked and crazy, clouds covering and then uncovering her, so warm and still. A woman on the beach should have silky fresh-pressed child's skin—pearly. Janelle's skin is wrinkled, lasso lines around her eyes, orange-tinted from tanning fluid. At night she feels twenty.

The heat is something awful, she has cotton-mouth … and suddenly, her dad is walking toward her on the sand—limping because of his bad toe. He is dead and so she smiles, it is good to know him. He looks annoyed, as though she's still a child with the flu, vomiting and sobbing.

He says, "Janelle, stop retching. There is only so much liquid."

First published in 52 | 250 – A Year of Flash

Meg Pokrass
Ecotherms (2021)

Today my husband is having the small black island on his back removed by a surgeon. The roots of the melanoma, the doctor says, are like mussels attached to a reef.

As surgeons snip away at his damage, sharks match their body temperatures to the water around them. There is the logic of ectotherms; how a body is nothing but heated rock. I'm at home in the quiet afternoon, waiting for a call from the hospital, remembering that sharks will surface while a seal is dreaming.

In my dream I ask him to marry me again, but only if the physiological variables change. I ask him by writing it on an old underwater photograph of myself taken in Maui ten years ago. I say, *this time, no variables.* I say, *this means we must dive down and visit the sharks, look them straight in their sleepy eyes while they circle the shells of our dreaming faces.*

Now I know what my father meant when he told me there's only so much liquid. How a person can't feel safe in the sea because crude oil keeps smothering starfish. In my dream, my husband attaches himself to my forehead while formulating a plan. I'm swimming around in my button-down sweater, monitoring my brainwave activity, trying to breathe.

Marty Brick
Adult Dark (2011)

"Kids," my aunt shouted from the back of the house. "Time to come in."

"Aw nuts. Already?" I complained but started back.

My cousin Lefty didn't move. "Come on, we'd better …" I began, but paused, looking to him for guidance.

He was right-handed, so his nickname was just the beginning of things that didn't quite make sense. Another was that he was younger than me, but clearly in change. But since I moved from the city to rural Indiana he helped acclimate me to wide-open playgrounds of cornfields and woods.

"First," he instructed, "don't say *aw nuts*. Who are you, Charlie Brown? Say *shit*. Say *damn*."

"Okay."

"Second. When were we told to go in?"

"When it's dark."

"Right. And is it dark?"

"I don't think it's dark." I believed this. It didn't seem dark. That was the other thing that was hard to get used to. We were right on the border of the time zone, so it got dark late. Mom would say, "It's bedtime," when just five miles to the west it was an hour until bedtime. Didn't make sense.

"This is adult dark. When you're inside drinking coffee, talking about sick people from church, sure it looks dark."

"It's not dark if you're in it," I told him.

"Exactly. You're learning."

"Boys. Come in." This time it was my mother. "It's dark."

We both giggled. We're far enough into the corn that she couldn't see us.

"You going in?" Lefty asked.

"Shit no," I told him.

First published in 52|250 – A Year of Flash

Marty Brick
Adult Dark (2021)

"Shit, those kids have been out there a long time."

"What's up?" Lefty asks and hands me another beer. I contemplate whether or not to crack it. Got the drive home in a while. I could ask the wife, but I hate that. There is always an undercurrent of "Yes, I'll cover your immaturity."

"I told the kids to come back when it was dark, but they're still out there."

"It's just adult dark. They'll be back. Have a cold one."

I look at the beer. Look at Lefty. One is worth it. I crack the can and say, "I think I'll wander out. See if I find them."

They're in the Indiana corn, pretending not to notice the time or light. Been there.

I'm 3 rows into the field and hear their voices, the glee of dissent. It's a good level of dark. Don't see anything until you're right upon it, but not total blackout. The level of light is exactly the same as the level of drunk I like.

And that's when I stumble upon Misty, Lefty's wife. "You looking for the kids?" she asks.

"Yep. But not too hard."

"Me neither," she says, lifting a wine glass. "Actually, me time." Then she lifts her shirt. "Or us time?"

In the distance I hear my son holler.

"What?" is all I can say.

"Lefty calls this adult dark. Are you an adult?"

The immediate answer was fairly easy, but the bigger question: what had I learned?

KM Elkes
Fair Weather (2014)

They had lain in bed the whole day. Now it was too late to go out.

"Let's pretend," he said.

She shifted under the duvet. "Where will we go?"

They looked at the ceiling, the filigree of cracks in the plaster that held all the journeys they might need.

"The seaside." He remembered she liked it there.

A tide-mark of ancient damp in the corner could be the ocean. They should take the scenic route, enjoy the view.

She played along for a while, then lost her way: "We're just following the rain."

She was American and thought he was obsessed with the weather. He said it was to do with being English, that he would teach her how. It was one of the things he had promised.

"We should have turned earlier," she said, as if he could control the filthy clouds, the hurtle of birds skimming the wind.

"There's bright sky over the coast," he said.

She wanted a break, but he said they should press on. They arrived to a green marble sea, white rollers coming in.

"It's cold," she said.

"Bracing," he said.

"I thought it would be better," she said.

"Let's make the most of it," he said.

Later, the street lamps outside the bedroom came on, casting the ceiling in a sallow light.

"Are you still awake?" he asked, but she didn't stir.

He dozed, imagining they were two shadows, walking towards the bright water until they reached the long, flat obstinacy of the sea wall.

First published in Lightship Anthology 3 *(Alma Books, 2014)*

KM Elkes
Clenched Yellow Feet
(2021)

My mother lay on the landing, smoking a cigarette. One of her slippers had tumbled down the stairs. It was keeled over like an old boat.

"Come up here, love." When she spoke, smoke curled from her nostrils. "I've something for you."

Halfway up the stairs were three china birds, nailed to the wall. She had bought them in a charity shop. Said they reminded her of holidays up north, long beaches under goose-coloured skies. There were only minor signs of damage—crackled glaze and chipped wing tips.

No-one had told her they should be pointing up, those birds, with their eager beaks. The white collar around their necks. Their clenched yellow feet.

"Don't worry," she said. The tip of her cigarette flared in the gloom. "I've got something special for you."

She wore her green dressing gown. Her hair was in heavy rollers, like a storm coming over her brow.

She took me to the beach once. There was a ship somewhere far out among the white tops. And a strong breeze. And sun enough to burn. Days later, she peeled sheets of wet, tender skin from my back. Like dragonfly wings, she said.

Her cigarette jabbed towards me. "Get up here. I'm not going to do anything."

As I passed the birds, I imagined them unpinned, swooping down the stairs, across the landing, out of the door. Chipped wings unfurled, necks stretched, and a single dot of light, shining from each eye.

Sam Rasnake
Postcards (2010)

To Duchamp
There are no tapestries here,
no weaving, no nights spent
undoing empires worth saving
We are glass & tubes & gears
that grind the wheels that turn
under a metal veil streaming
as if a single life—forgotten or
remembered—could be forged
in a blast of sand and steel
– New York, 1913

Amsterdam
Ssshhh—Don't tell anyone. I'm outside the hotel room
where Chet Baker died. What made him think he could fly?
I bribed the bellboy to let me in to see the window.
My fingers against the cool glass—the city, a cluster
of lights waiting for dawn, and suddenly I feel wings—
I swear—opening from both my shoulders.
See you soon. Maybe—
– 1994

To Buson

One crow walks the roof of a blue Mustang, speaks
to the sky, to nothing, speaks to hear his own voice
when it falls against gravel—Surely this winter,
from its wild and lonely places, will cover the hard
world in a breath, a shadow, in a moving on the wind.
He must know something, then hops down, disappears—
— 2006

Berlin
— for Edmund Kohler

The dust is everything. All times between
living and the dead blur to nothing, to one
foot in front of the other, to a slice of raw
potato, and water that hints at tea.
You should see this place. Dark hallways
with wrecked doors, empty stairwells where
music is silence. A broken city—Piles of
rubble here and here and here. So many.
— 1947

First published in 52 | 250 – A Year of Flash

Sam Rasnake
Postcards (2020)

To Diane
This then is the stain, the ugly truth
in cracked walls and peeled paint
The floor, a blur of grime
The only light, a paper lantern
in this delicious squalor of Eden
The couple kisses—or do they
She touches him—or does she

The eyes are always present, searching
for connection, for the impossible thread,
something to anchor this ache of waking,
to feel without feeling, to shame the shame
– N.Y.C. 1966

Chicago, the Earl of Old Town
– for John Prine, with Hello—if you say it

Sometimes the words don't come. They hide—
too true too caring too unwilling—as if to say
by not saying. There are holes with no bottom,
skies that are nothing but cloud. Sometimes

the hard truth is a wrinkle in my stomach, an ache
where nothing is, a stare through the closed window.
We can whisper: he is gone, she is gone—but
that never tells the whole story, does it?

Maybe we *can* do without doing. Maybe so.
Or at least know the stars are listening.
– 1971

        … a reply:

> *From my table, the morning*
> *in hand with coffee steam –*
> *almost as if I willed it,*
> *the pileated woodpecker,*
> *large and mystical, floats*
> *to the cherry's trunk,*
> *an effortless beauty,*
> *a special moment of good*
> *on such dark days, then goes.*
>
>   *– April 2020*

Paris

– for Gerda

"a grub … waiting to become a butterfly"

This then: the slipping of the self
into another—a sleekness as
it oozes over the soul—

The beast of want swallowing
the eyes and swell
of life—It's the body

dreamed, burning, touched
in the darkness
of one hot summer
– 1924

Chelsea Biondolillo
Safari Club, Estacada, Oregon, circa 1979 (2011)

Our knives and forks clatter against the simple white plates. Over my grandfather's shoulder, a leopard is frozen in mid-leap, his chipped claws sinking into a gazelle. The gazelle has been painted with red stripes to heighten the illusion of split-second predation.

I always ask to walk the perimeter of the restaurant. My grandmother takes my hand and we headfirst through the Arctic, where ermines, captured behind glass, are stuck forever half white. The walrus head seems impossibly large. She hoists me up so I can rub my fingers across his hard muzzle, play the whiskers like strings on a ukulele. Then under the jaguars leaping above the dance floor. The killing isn't worrisome to me—the blood is paint, the postures of fear and survival, all posed. The hunter is long dead, too.

Back in the Serengeti, a lion carries an antelope in his mouth while a hyena menaces from across the glass case behind my chair. Dik-diks and warthogs edge the display, watching the drama unfold, presumably. The lion is dusty, and there is a cobweb between the "limp" antelope legs.

My grandfather saws through his Swiss steak while my grandmother navigates her Monte Cristo into and out of her raspberry jam. She dabs a red spot on her blouse with the corner of her napkin that's been dipped in her ice water. I get the fisherman's platter and devour everything but the oysters. We eat languidly, while hundreds of dull eyes look on.

First published in 52|250 – A Year of Flash

Chelsea Biondolillo
Safari Club, Estacada, Oregon, 2017 (2020)

The first thing I did when I got back was look for the Safari Club. This town was never supposed to be my home, but here I am, picking trash out of my grandparent's yard, which is now mine, already wondering what to do about the brambles.

But the windows were boarded and caution tape wrapped around the sidewalks, mid-demolition. I'd wanted to show my boyfriend. It's something I used to do with boyfriends, back when I lived in the nearby city. I'd bring them out here, past the winding river curves, through the firs and past farms and empty yellow squares that used to be farms.

Then, through the second light on the highway, onto Broadway. We'd park on the street, under the fake thatched roof, in front of a plate glass window full of taxidermied lions or leopards. I'd watch their faces when we walked through the doors, confronted first by the grizzly and polar bears, then after a hard left into the lounge, the hundreds of other animals, posed, mounted, displayed. I wanted to see their expression; learn what all the death and artifice inspired in them.

I wanted to know if they worried about the animals or the hunter.

Now, the Safari Club is gone like my grandparents and there's a Dollar Store in its place. You can't learn anything from a Dollar Store except how little a person is willing to get by with—a person, or a whole town.

Maggie Sokolik

Brown Paper (2010)

The manager complains that the closet shelves are lined with newspaper. She has instructed the front desk clerk to affix proper paper to each of the empty shelves.

Bharadwaj stands with his back to me, scraping off the yellowed pages of the *Ganashakti*. He then begins measuring, cutting, and gluing brown paper from a long roll. He sings in Bengali. The manager enters to inspect his work. After a short discussion, he says, "Yes, Madam," removes the paper from the bottom shelf, remeasures, recuts, and reglues.

The telephone is a mere prop on the desk. It is not connected to a wire, the wall, or the outside world. The small hard cots are covered in graying sheets, naked of blankets. A trail of ants creeps along the grout in the shower, going from nowhere to nowhere. The little red fridge humming in the corner is empty except for one Kingfisher beer, supplied by Bharadwaj.

"Americans like beer, right?" he asks. "It's not acceptable for a woman to buy beer." He proffers the beer in a brown paper bag.

The window stands open in hopes of a breeze, but diesel fumes and dust drift in instead. I think I hear a monkey, but Bharadwaj says it's just an ordinary bird. I want to hear monkeys.

The shelves are completed. I run my hands over the clean dry surface of the fresh paper.

"Beautiful," I whisper.

I have nothing to put there.

First published in 52 | 250 – A Year of Flash

Maggie Sokolik
Sagarmatha (2021)

The Simpsons theme plays from my phone. I grab it, pacing my room, ready for another day. Training young Nepalis about online business. My company's sent me here for a three-month session.

"There's a strike—no cabs," Abhik, my handler, says. "Working on it." He clicks off.

The day before, a thirty-something looked up from his notebook and asked, "Why are we doing this?"

I pasted on my biggest smile and filled my mouth with platitudes, then stopped. "Maybe, someday," I shrugged. He returned to his notebook.

A text: I can borrow scooters.

"Hard pass," I text back, picturing the dirt track into the Himalayas.

Another twenty minutes elapse as I sip tea and watch the slow-moving river off the deck.

A pickup arrives—Abhik and the driver in front. I throw my things in back and squeeze in on the bench seat.

As we bounce up the track, I ask Abhik about the strike.

"A general one—about everything. You're not a nervous type, are you?"

"Why?"

"That bridge." He points. "They just removed a bomb. One person hurt—it exploded when they defused it."

"How will we get to the airport later?"

"The strike should be over. We'll hire a car. We'll see Sagarmatha if we leave early. You know, Everest."

I've been here a month and I still haven't seen Everest.

S J Mannion
Redemption Song (2014)

I met a man. Initially, he seemed a loud, talkative man, full of argument. But there is something quiet about him too. I find quietness appealing. Particularly, in a man. Yes, it is there, behind his words and in his hands. There is a stillness and a calm about his hands. Though large, they are well shaped and beautiful. Laying on his lap when seated, they rest there, priest-like and pale, the skin rubbed smooth and thin by time, the veins royal blue and visible. I picture them often.

He is an artist and though I have a healthy disrespect for artists – having once been a constantly auditioning muse – it is because of this I imagine his hands to be closely linked to his true self. I believe in the integrity of his hands, in the truth of them. I imagine their touch, his touch, to be a kind of blessing. As touch is or can be. An acknowledgement. A wordless, silent comfort. Perhaps the best we have to give.

I met a man. And on simply being interested in him, I am rejuvenated. I am reminded of who I was, and am, and still could be. I am reminded of the eternal promise of encounter, and of course, the tenacity of hope. I am reminded that even now, perhaps especially now – I still believe in love. I still believe that each one can be centred in two. I still believe in the whole damn story.

First published in Open Pen Magazine

S J Mannion
Island Woman (2021)

It must have been cold when she went into the water.

They found her body three weeks later. The currents carried her as she knew they would, far away.

It's been years and only now do we begin to speak of her. I still feel unentitled to the measure of my grief. Being a cuckoo in that nest.

That last weekend, we spoke of our mutual love of water and of our island nature. Of the width and depth of the oceans and seas and their never ending possibilities.

We spoke of the sense of renewal, of rebirth, water brings. And then contrary to this, of the improbability of true personal change. She said she had begun to think on absence as more beneficial than presence.

In retrospect I wish I had argued this point. She was saying goodbye to me then. But I am glad that she felt she could.

I see her framed in the doorway as I left. Smiling. Still I let her go. I waved. What else could I do?

And now, though I wish she were still in the world, that she had stayed, though I am forever lonelier without her, I am comforted that she chose her death as she could not chose her life, that she sought and found the support of water. It eases me to think of her in the arms of the ocean, cradled in the deep.

Though it must have been cold when she went in to the water.

Gary Percesepe
Wordkill (2011)

In the room you are the absence of room. You are the nothing in my life that wants to become something. At the circus you are the flyer and I am the catcher but there is no circus. You won't jump but I wait anyway. Religion helps. Today someone said: If you meet the Buddha on the road kill him. I'd kill your husband if you hadn't already. I was four the first time I was killed. My brother walked me home a birthday cake; the next week he was asphyxiated. You always remember your first. Next up: my sister. My father lashed her to the banister for protesting the war. She whimpered softly all night. I snuck her Ritz crackers and a bowl of water. I tried to read my father's knots but could not. She reached a cracked hand up to me. I took her hand and kissed it. Then I left. I died again that night but really who keeps track. You heard your parents' hateful speech for decades. We had the good sense to avoid the L word for a time. I cracked first. But you could have. That's the thing right there. There is always somewhere to fall from. We couldn't remember who saved whom. Then you got ill and wouldn't tell me. It wasn't fair but I understood. You wanted me to kill you again. So I did. I had help. I've always been lucky that way. Now she's dead too.

First published in 52 | 250 – A Year of Flash

Gary Percesepe
In Rome (2021)

That summer I waited for Gabriella in a dingy *pensione* near the Spanish Steps. I'd sent a ticket. But I knew she wouldn't come, though she had said she would. Someone called one night, and I heard the manager of the *pensione* call my name. I picked up the phone. Rome is a city built to erase time, seven layers of ruin beneath its current mystery. A city with the power to erase time, or, like the Foreign Legion, to erase a past life. Like a metronome, Rome tick-tocks, its beat regular and eternal but also pointless since time has stopped forever. The path of our lives is riddled with gaps in our memory. Whether they are actual lapses or whether we avoid thinking of certain things, certain events, is unclear. Would it help you to know where I am now? What does chronological time mean in love? Pictures from that summer show Gabriella small and tan in strappy rose sandals garnished with silver. A face in black and white that I would barely recognize in the streets surrounding the Spanish Steps or seated by the *porte-cochère* in front of the building where I wait. Hot leaves from plane trees fall dead to the ground on the banks of the Tiber. What other details are required? Suppose I told you I hold the phone to my ear to listen? I hear the crackling of static grow louder and louder. It keeps us from hearing a voice calling from far away.

Diane Brown
A Rat in the Wardrobe
(2012)

Despite her space reduced to bed, chair, wardrobe and bedside cabinet of three drawers, the untidiness she's lived with her whole life has made itself at home. Out of the drawers, I fish squares of unwrapped chocolate, plastic bags, magazines rich with the lives of strangers and torn out pieces of newspaper, clippings they'd be called if she possessed scissors. Scissors and knives are banned here, and the doors are locked, just in case.

"That's our old house," Mum says, pointing to a picture of an upmarket inner-city house, the backyard resplendent with pool and outdoor kitchen.

"Done up, of course." The street is right but not the number.

A few weeks ago, I drove past our old state house, finding it unchanged, though the rubbish dump over the fence that reeked on a hot day has been buried beneath a park more suited to the area's gentrification. The last time I was able to take Mum out I asked her if she wanted to see it. "Never," she said. "I hated that house."

After the drawers I tackle the wardrobe, throwing out unrelated socks, doll-sized t-shirts, and the hand-knitted cardigan that took 25 years to finish, now matted and shrunken in the hot water laundry.

"Take what you want," Mum says. "I don't go out now, so I don't need much."

"They won't fit me either," I say, and she pinches my waist.

"Oh, you have put on weight."

I escape to the shops and buy hangers.

"Now when I come back," I say, "I want to find this wardrobe still tidy." Easy to think our roles have been reversed but Mum was never a hypocrite, never urged me to tidy my room.

"Not my fault," Mum says. "There's a rat in the wardrobe. Chewed its way up through the floor." Her face is straight.

Not for the first time, I wonder if she really has lost it. She was always difficult to read.

Diane Brown
Visiting My Mother's Grave (2021)

My mother is dead for four years now. I visited her family grave the other day in the city where I grew up. The cemetery is up the road from the house my father built. I often walked through it, though my mother didn't like me to, even when I was grown up with my own children. Perhaps she felt the weight of all those bodies lying close to us. We dropped her ashes and those of her younger brother and sister into the hole cut in the concrete. Their names were inscribed on a new plaque. Anyone seeing the dates of siblings who died within three months of each other might conclude that they died from some infectious disease. Nothing so dramatic, just old age, and once my mother had given them the cue, they might have thought, *Why not?*

My aunt and uncle had their own urns. Mum's were in a plastic bag. My younger brother lay over the grave and poured her out. I thought it lacked dignity, but he said she always wanted to go back into the dirt and there was no way he was leaving her encased in plastic. Part of her is encased in glass with my father in a handcrafted paperweight sitting on my desk. A teaspoon of each of their ashes mixed and swirling in a silvery spiral. A thing of beauty or possibly a good weapon to throw at someone's head should I be invaded.

I patted the grave, said, "Hello, Mum," and was surprised to find myself on the verge of tears. I forgot to say hello to the others, but I did say, "I hope you are all getting along. I wish I could tell you everything I've found out about our family since you left." I didn't say anything else apart from goodbye.

I'm not sure ashes can hear. I never talk to the paperweight either.

Cherise Wolas
Things I Should
Have Done #1 (2011)

I should have left my ex-husband at the altar after the screaming match we had the day before we married. A fight so vicious I still recall my fingernails scraping the dark hardwood as I tucked my head between my knees, imagining how horrid to be a battered woman with a Ph.D. The day before our wedding I was curled like a comma in our new dining room, with wrought iron light fixtures like torture devices from the Middle Ages. A place I hadn't wanted but he had, because, he said, my apartment was "too you," by which I decided he actually meant we needed more space to live in extraordinary happiness. When I agreed to move, I imagined this large old duplex, with our first bedroom together, would be a haven, filled with sunny sex on Sundays, crunching on Butterfinger bars naked in bed, creating our gorgeous future story. The apartment I left for him had clean lines, varnished pale wooden floors, whitewashed nooks and crannies, noisy birds in the rubber tree outside the bedroom window. That apartment called to me the day before we wed. Crushed into the corner, behind the table, fearing an actual blow, I imagined being back home again, snailed in a pale grey suede chair, staring out into the black night, sipping Pernod on the rocks, listening to soaring music in the star-dusted room, still yearning for the day we would wed.

First published in 52|250 – A Year of Flash

Cherise Wolas
Sailing (2021)

Stacy and her skiff and her teensy bikini and we were sixteen and
the Italian merchant marines climbing aboard were on leave after
six months at sea. I wanted dry land, then was pleased to be
sailing—the flirting, the anodyne kisses with older handsome
strangers. Then it was night, a scarred table, a cheap glass ashtray
that read *Jolly Roger Motel: The Place For Fun.* I watched Mario
sucking Stacy's huge breasts. Saw him swollen and uncut—I knew
the difference. Stacy twisted it and his eyes rolled up to heaven.
Luigi watched me watching them, then cursed in angry rapid
Italian when I stared out at the moonlit night. A groan, I looked—
Stacy sealed to the tip before swallowing Mario down. Sitting on
the motel stairs, I wished for I don't know what. Since that night,
I've permitted only danger I create myself. And I didn't know
anything about her life until she turned into a reality TV star
during the pandemic. I watched an episode. The plastic surgery
hadn't made her pretty. All these years passing the Jolly Roger
Motel, I never thought about her, though I always think about
the teenage girl in *The Painted Bird,* raped with a Coke bottle in
a sunny field, and about Italian Luigi, imagining him married, the
father of daughters, wondering if he remembers that long-ago
split-second when he felt misled, cheated, and didn't grapple a
teenaged girl onto that other queen bed with its rusted spread.

Catherine McNamara
Tales from Bodri Beach
(2011)

This is how it is. Miranda rises early and goes to the beach wearing a green shirt over her bikini, barefoot. She leaves Leo in thick sleep, dew at his mouth. Leo is half-aware of Miranda kneeling in the tent tying up her bikini, and when she is gone he rolls over sensing the summons of a new dream. He consciousness wavers, then comes apart as a series of dishevelled constellations. In the north, on a local bus savagely ridden around hairpin bends, their daughter Manou wishes she had stayed in Paris. Hot, regretful, she unravels a scarf that dances from the window and becomes lifeless in the dirt. As close as they are to the coast, the land breathes warm flames.

Miranda walks down the track to the water. She thinks of Leo and strides into the waves. She kicks away, her face shifting across the water's hem. She tips onto her back as the soundless gulf pulls away, hears the whine of a boat. At the first buoy she stops, checking the vessel has headed off. She can see the camping ground with its pageant-like spread of tents. She can't see their blue triangle, or the red one-man tent she has put up for her daughter Manou. She dunks under to see seams crafted in the sand, the vista extending to a rubbery blue. Beneath her, the buoy chain sways down to a cluster of bricks like a burial mound.

First published in Lakeview, International Journal of Literature and Arts

Catherine McNamara
Propellor (2021)

It is August and I am swimming in Lago di Garda while my parents have gone off into the *pineta* into the trails of their argument, Papà following, mother stomping ahead in her printed bikini with orange paillettes. My name is Serena. I am back-floating, taught by my French grandfather who this morning was driven back to his nursing home over the alps, crying and pawing the glass. Domenico is my father. I hear his raised voice from the *pineta*, but I know they will go afterwards for drinks. I smell the pine trees as though I am crouched there, gathering cones.

Tomorrow you will read about me. The girl on the northern rim of the lake, struck by two German tourists in a motorboat cutting close to the shore, where one of them last summer made love with an Italian barmaid, he thinks, under those trees before the pontoon.

The way the boat pushes my head under is a rolling surge, and then the propeller scrolls through my leg, cleaner than a shark. I will survive. My schoolfriends perform a vigil. But nobody can carry on a vigil for the months I am vegetal, pressed under a quilt of waves. One boy draws the mountains above the lake, and the way these peaks are throbbing and torn makes the teacher advise him to try again, though she cannot say why.

I recover. My grandfather is dead. My parents look at the flattened bedsheet beneath my knee, arms shelved together.

Erik Kennedy

The Personal Responsibility Model of Wildlife Conservation (2016)

There are as many species on earth as there are Austrians (8.7 million). Ours is a time of personal responsibility. What can't be achieved by an individual who subordinates destiny to willpower? Let's assign one species to each Austrian. That species must be kept alive on pain of death. Expect campaigns, appeals, initiatives, programmes, directives, operations, and schemes. Don't be surprised by the vigour and ingenuity of the private sector when a problem has got to be solved. Endangered Austrians, Near Threatened Austrians, and Austrians of Least Concern can all agree. And would we be so cavalier about extincting a type of (for example) prawn if twinkly, sandy-haired Jochen has to die for it? The answer may still be yes, but whatever we say in public instead of yes will have to convince Jochen's brooding, thunder-browed friends.

First published in Ohio Edit

Erik Kennedy
Soft Power (2021)

The invention of practical brainwave-to-speech technology had a knock-on effect that no one seemed to have anticipated. Animals now could not only 'speak', but they proved to be vastly more entertaining than humans. The earliest interviews immediately showed this. We had underestimated their intelligence, of course, but also their wit and persuasiveness. All animals appeared to have hidden depths. An otter named Seòlta could tell thousands of coruscating jokes. A clip of a lemur fact-checking and humiliating a respected journalist became the most-viewed video in history.

The human monopoly on expression had been broken and, as usually happens in such cases, the market was transformed. It wasn't just that animal media was novel and interesting. That drew people in, yes, but they stayed because of the punch of the storytelling, the giddy and deranged excesses of the humour. Animals became bona fide stars and important artists, and the legal and financial professions predictably evolved to manage their rights and assets.

The longer the animal arts flourished, the greater the soft power of animals became. They were oracles, troubadours, bards, soothsayers, heartthrobs. They were known for what they gave to the world, not for what they took from it. Schoolchildren, when polled, said they wanted to grow up to be animals.

And people wondered if that soft power would stay soft. Humans knew what they had used power for, and no one was sure yet if it could be used for anything else.

Stephen Hastings-King
The Past (2011)

I remember at the top of the path from the footbridge over the multi-colored river in the basement of the house there was a collection of seashells arranged in transparent polyurethane cubes stacked with an eccentric sense of geometry into a 3-dimensional map of an imaginary sea. Aquarium paraphernalia has been placed around the map to enable a functioning ecosystem.

I remember the cavernous sense of empty gymnasium and the sense that I had interrupted something invisible and secret.

I remember being a commando wielding a plastic gun on the roof of the high school until the police came with weapons drawn. I yelled "It's plastic" again and again, still not understanding the situation.

I remember becoming other people.

First published in 52 | 250 – A Year of Flash

Stephen Hastings-King
Interval (2021)

In the interval, I would sometimes remember walking the footbridge rail over a river of paint, holding my arms out to keep my balance past where you could hold onto the cable: but the memory must have been of a dream; I am afraid of heights.

In the interval, the man who lived in the house at the top of the hill passed away: his three-dimensional map of an imaginary sea, along with the aquarium paraphernalia that allowed its inhabitants to breathe, were scattered across the region via the mechanism of an estate sale.

In the interval, maybe ghosts would still come and go in the unused gymnasium over the memorial to the Civil War dead than named them: maybe it's still there.

In the interval, from time to time, I hear from my friend, the other rooftop commando on the high school that night: we talk vaguely about getting a bourbon but we never do.

In the interval, I have rarely gone back: one time I walked a peat bog with Martian acres of carnivorous flora; at the entrance was an ancient, weathered wooden sign that had been put up after I left; I stopped in front of the house where I grew up & remembered the telephone number; someone asked what I was doing there; I couldn't say.

Michelle Elvy
A Knobby Thing (2010)

She reclines in her window seat, sees the starboard prop whirring superfast, looking slo-mo. She closes her eyes and drifts back to yesterday, the last day of everything, 80-hour work-weeks, devoted dull boyfriend, pet cat (a gift) whom she secretly hates. She brings her thumb to teeth, gnaws where there's nothing left to gnaw, sorrowful nails bitten down to nothing. She feels ugly but ready for anything.

The wheels touch down and she gathers her things, spits cuticle out the side of her mouth, *thp*. She steps out into air so hot she's sure she'll never be able to breathe here. Then she inhales deeply and instead of feeling oxygen hitting lungs, she *tastes* it— floral and citrus, sweaty and sweet. The first breath is as miraculous and jarring as the one she took some thirty-three years back. She almost cries out, too: the punch of this new world hits her hard.

She wanders along Main Street, spots the trademarked arches garish and gold against this landscape, jutting up amongst dusty buildings and peeling paint—an echo of her old world. She longs for its familiar cool, then spies a small market across the street. Locals laugh, handle fruits she's never seen or heard of. She goes to the first long table, eyeballs a knobby thing, large and green, asks a dark woman with droopy breasts and happy eyes, "Qu'est-ce que c'est?" The woman answers, "Breadfruit, love." She picks it up, smiles, thinks she'll give it a try.

First published in 52 | 250 – A Year of Flash

Michelle Elvy

Squall (2021)

Do you remember when blue and black were just blue and black? This crayon: an ocean, a sky, a marble, an eye. Here, black: that sheep, or night. Orange and pink: bubblegum sunsets. Red: fire under your skin and in your heart.

*

When we were kids, we cut out shapes just the right size for our small hands. We glued them down, some neat, some not. Teacher scolded, sometimes:

> *Draw inside the lines,*
> *make your letters slant*

We painted glue on our fingers, let it harden, bent it off in long sticky strands, smooth, translucent. Once, you peeled a piece away and it looked ghosty-grey like a ship. We said we'd sail across oceans—me as star navigator and you with clouds in your eyes.

*

But what of grey? Clouds build in towering heights, touch down on the horizon; the line between blackening sky and purpling frothing sea, a sheet of rain connecting them. The air acid, anticipation electric.

We said we'd build a boat and in our dreams we believed it.

Rachmaninoff rain pounds the sea flat. From behind the magnificent skies, the sun may shine through, glowing like a god.

We
said
our boat
would sail any
sea, with any wind,
and we cut out triangle
shapes, pasted them on the
grey classroom wall where they
floated all
year long.

SLEEP
VIEWS
THE
WORLD

Al McDermid
Sleep the Ferryman (2010)

Sleep views the world at right angles and has never seen a rainbow. He lives by the river where he was once a ferryman, in a shack that he built from railroad ties, orange crates, and old typewriters. The shack is not plumb and groans in the wind. When it rains, he sits under its tin roof and listens to the symphony. Sometimes it plays Chopin, other times, Beethoven. He wishes it would play more Mahler, but the roof never plays the same piece twice. He thinks that were he to get a new roof, maybe he could hear some of his favorites one more time.

Sleep once took passengers across the river for a price. He might ask for food, or a fishing fly, or a fool-me-once, but he'd take almost anything as long as the name of that thing began with 'f'. He traded these for the other letters that he needed. A German tourist once offered his wife, who in turn offered to set fire to the shack. When Sleep declined her offer, she suggested a fusillade. Sleep took them for free; they fought with each other all the way across.

When anyone took Sleep's ferry, they'd get to the other side, but it could be anywhere on the other side. That was before the rains stopped and river dried up. Sleep now just sits in his shack, waiting to hear Mozart.

First published in 52 | 250 – A Year of Flash

Al McDermid
The River with No Bridge (2021)

While on his way to his idea of California, Trout came to a river with no bridge. There had once been a bridge, but it had been washed away in a famous flood. The river didn't look large enough to have hosted a major flood, but the bridge had been replaced with a plaque commemorating the event, so it must have been. Which was no doubt a great comfort to those who had tragically lost their lives, but of little use to anyone wanting to cross the river.

Toward sunset, as Trout was contemplating under which tree he might bed down for the night, he came to a clearing where he found a cowboy sitting on a log next to a fire pit, poking at the fire with a stick.

"You're just in time," the cowboy said, looking up from his fire, a flurry of sparks obscuring his face.

Trout stared at him blankly. The cowboy had a hawk-like face and drooping mustache and looked vaguely familiar, so Trout thought perhaps he had wandered into a western movie and forgotten his lines.

"Excuse me?" Trout said.

The cowboy gestured across the river with his chin. Trout looked to see clouds as black as the bat–lightning hair of the girl who had once stolen his heart gathering in the distance. Trout suspected it was a sign or omen, but he didn't know of what. Instead, he thought about the girl with the bat–lightning hair, a girl far away.

Gail Ingram
Whispers (2015)

A rabbit pops out of a hole. A mangy hare, in fact, her eyes glassy, looking for escape.

She has six kits in the warren below. Their fur is mangy too, stiff. Death is on her tongue, a taste that seems to come from inside, rather than, say, some dropped poisoned carrot, blanched like the landscape.

The wind catches the willows out left. There. She bounds from the dust-bowl entrance. Darts left, right, her gait uneven. Stops as suddenly as she began. Here. Her coat blends tan-grey into tussock. Her nose quivers, for the first time, her eyes look interested.

Dark clouds press the horizon. A rumble. The hills look closer. Watch. They open like a walnut-shell cracks. And the ground, where the hare sits, blows like breath.

The horizon has split. Two nut-halves. Lightening crackles between the broken hill. A crack begins to run across the earth towards the hare. Her whole being shifts towards it; her ears lean into it, she trembles. The crack has singular direction, and tussock, stone, tree fall into its wake.

It travels more quickly than you think. She reacts now. Uses her hind legs to propel herself. For a moment she is high above the crack. Her fur is no longer dull but sleek, her front-legs reach skyward, she is in motion.

We can remember her like this. We don't need to imagine the rush downwards towards the open earth into crumbling, crunching mineral. Let us recall her fine last leap towards her kittens.

First published in Flash Frontier: An Adventure in Short Fiction

Gail Ingram
After the ground stopped shaking (2021)

the mountains sighed and shook their heads. A grasshopper leapt into her brain. She felt skittish. Aware of everything that had ever happened to her: the cry of gull overhead, calling for its mother; her brother learning to drive, the look of intensity on his face; falling from the jungle gym, that moment when you don't know how it will end, then you do. The pantry was on the floor. Marjoram scattered over chili sauce over everything. But that was 10 years ago when the city went up in dust. This was only a truck passing the medical centre. The claustrophobia of the walls. People breathing. The endless movement of fish in the tank. What was the point of memory anyway? The parts of the brain we did use lit up on a screen like a constellation; would it all scatter and shift when the dark bubbled up, no longer shaped by meaning? Really, the whole world was chaos, though nobody wanted to know. And especially not her; she was too young. And the doctor calling her name.

Michael Parker
Ghost Searches Downtown (2011)

I walked to the bakery where we used to buy our weekly bread. I meandered through parking lots looking for our mini-van. I searched the faces in the grocery store trying to see Elle. Does she search the passing faces for a resemblance of me?

I scoped out the city park, gazing at the faces of the children on the playgrounds. Do any of them have my eyes or smile? I visited the city library and then haunted the entrances of our restaurants, theaters, and farmer's market.

Despondent, and not remembering the way home, I took to the heart of the city. The streets and sidewalks were furiously alive. Cars were out in droves, passing to and fro like angry bees. People strolled by in faceless crowds, like giant flurries of storms crossing the valley with the saintly demeanor of purple-robed priests entering Communion.

I looked imploringly at the people approaching me. I held out my hands like a beggar. Each hand held a photo of my wife or kids. "Excuse me, have you seen my family?"

I knew that if just one person would look at the photos, they might recognize one of the faces and that would awaken a memory in them, and then that memory would become a story that they could tell. And then that story might be one of the missing stories that would fill part of my hungry void. But no one looked at me, nor even noticed me. No one told a story.

First published in 52 | 250 – A Year of Flash

Michael Parker
Ghost Returns Home (2021)

The winter storm has settled above me like a dark continent, aubergine and gray. It has eaten the moon and her children. The oracles, because of this, are choked and diminished.

Following the lonely roads, I have finally found my way home. The house of the hush and hush is set askew. Elle and the kids are missing, and the portals stationed in the mirrors and dark tapestries on the wall are thrown open to the other distant regions, even to the Underworld.

At its core, the thin threads of light are swallowed. I can hear the cumbrous lullabies of Night's naked shades: the shadows that stick fast to their dim places as if waiting for friends or loved ones. In these surroundings, I fear not. This is my home and Night is soft and gathers me roundly in her obsidian wings.

Pacing the rooms and halls tonight, I look at myself in passing windows and mirrors. I am thinner, a ghost of my former days. My lungs are full of stones. To draw a breath, I must draw in the circumference of the moon.

A shade catches my eye in a mirror. Long as the room, crooked, cadaverous, he is drawn and pale, as if his cloak were the weave of shadows behind dead trees, from the hideous corners of haunted halls or an ailing evening. Reality strikes me: I have known this solitary apparition my entire life. It is me.

Abha Iyengar
The Price (2010)

She could not force times of entry and exit. She could only watch from behind the screen. The work was delicate, they had to ingest very carefully, just those areas of memory in which Moshe's fears resided. She could see them undergoing change, ingesting more and more, cowering in corners, not wanting to move. Some of them still flitted about, unaffected, exiting to enter again. But many of them were slowly congealing into live carcasses, staring into death.

Though she had hardly known her father then, she just wanted Moshe to return to her the way he was before captivity.

The Academy had given her a choice, pay for physical reconstruction or mental, she could not have both. Moshe would return to his former self, the horrors of his incarceration removed from his memory. She would touch his limp leg, his cavernous cheek, his broken mouth and see a father's love in his eyes again.

They were working hard, identifying and drawing into themselves the micro morsels that were Moshe's all-encompassing scenes of hell. She wrung her hands as she watched them falling at a faster pace into the corners, creating a litter of nothing much, just a vast collection of tiny proboscises, a surreal painting of sorts.

Soon, none would leave and she could not force them, nor sweep them out.

She would have to live with them in her own home. Maybe she could lock them up, once she got Moshe.

First published in Tapas, Issue 58, Doorknobs & Bodypaint

Abha Iyengar
The Return (2021)

She got Moshe with only those parts of his brain alive that remembered joy and the wisdom of his time. She locked up what remained of his fears in a room and soundproofed it, so that no one would hear their screams as they writhed in agony, remembering the torture of the concentrations camps where Moshe had once been incarcerated.

Her mother had escaped to America with her as a small child and then died within a few years. She excelled in school and found a well-paying job. Living frugally, working hard, she amassed wealth. She could not forget her father and was sure he was alive.

After years of relentless searching, she found him in The Academy in Germany, where they were experimenting with memory and body politics.

On her insistence of having her father back, they said they could return him either physically able or mentally sound. She had to choose and she did. They used their methods to extricate from his mind all harmful, fear-filled memory.

For ten years, she nursed him alone. Moshe's lifeless body declined but she recorded his every whisper. The books he recalled, the hymns he sang. He would be remembered.

As she saw his mouth quiver for the last time with a whispered melody, her voice rose in song.

His eyes closed and he slumped over the side of the bed, his paper body disintegrating into tiny skins that flew around in the air, twirling to her song, then quietly settling.

Tina Barry
Bride and Groom (2011)

At the flea market where we buy candles shaped like fairies and soap that wafts patchouli, sits a man in a wheelchair. He wears an old black tux, shiny at the elbows, and his gray hair has been styled and sprayed into a fragile tornado. On his lap sits a Chihuahua wearing a bridal outfit—veil and all. No one seems to notice the couple, except us. We can't stop staring at them staring into each other's eyes, so much in love.

First published in 52 | 250 – A Year of Flash

Tina Barry
Dog Psychic (2021)

Lucy centers the sign "Dog Psychic and Past Life Regressionist" on her folding table and sits, content to sip tea and nod at the regulars. Beside her, she's erected a screen to shield a pet-sized loveseat, made comfortable with embroidered pillows.

Squinting between the constellation of vendors, she notices a woman with an old Lab. The dog's heartsick, she thinks, observing its drooping head, the plodding, joyless walk. She isn't surprised when the woman, spotting Lucy, hurries to her table.

"Hannah's depressed," the woman says, nodding to the dog that rolls on its back, one paw covering its eyes. Nothing she's tried—St. John's Wort, licorice root, even, she admitted, an organic sirloin—has alleviated the dog's sadness.

Lucy kneels before the dog. "Come, Hannah," she says, taking the dog's leash.

As Hannah reclines, Lucy leans over, places her hands on its silken head. Lifetimes of longing pass through her stinging fingertips. Images begin to flow. There's Hannah, a puppy, her fur a glistening ink blot in the sun. A man had loved the dog, though briefly; she feels the heat of his hands as he strokes the pup's belly.

There's not much Lucy can offer the dog but a lie. "He has not forgotten you," she says, remembering her own hair untouched by gray, a blouse embroidered with violets, and the man who lifted it over her head and pulled her to his chest.

Anna Nazarova-Evans
The Coat (2013)

There she is, Elvie, wearing all my clothes whilst I stand here in the rain. The glass between us is thick. The blue dress on her is a piece of Honolulu sky Dave brought back from a sunny beach. The wet patch on my shoulder is getting bigger.

They delivered her earlier today. Dave used a pen knife to cut through the duct tape on the box. Her plastic flesh exuded a faint but distinct smell. Dave stripped me naked and used the clothes to dress her carefully as if she was a new-born.

"There we go, old girl," he said throwing a water rat coat over my shoulders. A patch of dust and dead moths quickly formed around my feet. He placed Elvie in the best position in the shop window before ringing Simon.

"I'll leave it outside for you," he said down the phone.

Simon must have forgotten about the coat, so here I am in front of my ghost-like reflection. He is sure to pick me up in the morning. It will have stopped raining. He will put me under his armpit and carry me like a log across the road in front of Elvie's eyes. The wet fur will glisten in the sun the same way it did when the rat wore it. It will make me feel like I too have been alive once. The top of the coat will flap open bearing my breasts, but I won't be ashamed—they're only plastic.

Anna Nazarova-Evans
Space Dust (2021)

The air was so sharp, we watched our words evaporate. Staying in bed with her all day was heaven, but Elvie tricked me with promises of free booze and "treats" when we get to the dancefloor. Getting out from under the duvet was like floating into cosmos. We both wanted to be Valentina Tereshkova – the first woman into space. Except that I always thought about how lonely she must have been out there in her tiny shuttle.

Moon breath enwrapped planes flying above us as we stood in the queue to the club. Elvie laughed at me, because I said our drunken conversation wasn't deep enough. Something brewed in my guts, an old string yearning to be plucked. Feelings collected into a drop, about to let go under its amassed weight. Her lips brushed my ear as she whispered something to me, pushing me against the wall. I wanted to keep her warmth, so I pressed my lips against hers and imagined her taste melting into me. This could have lasted a lightyear or a second. Then she pulled back and said, "What the hell, Polly?"

Someone laughed in the queue behind us and we shuffled along, her talking about the housing market, me counting the cigarette butts on the ground.

The awkwardness reverberated like a tuning fork as we walked through the entrance. When I saw her put her arms around Dave's neck, I was a dust particle fired into the infinite cold sky.

Darryl Price

The Sleepwalker as Map, the Map as Sleepwalker
(2010)

It doesn't matter what was in the middle. It took each and every one by the nose hairs anyway from where we were standing but didn't disappear us, except as one ink might disappear dissolving into another. We stained each other's lives, squirting like grape juice. Even the breakdown of the precious paper molecules appeared to be just another secretly written out chart to unknown locations just outside the present situation's experience. Sometimes the map presents itself as you go. Look. All you had to do was to walk quietly deeper and deeper into the places that you dreamed of until you arrived back in your own hometown, another summer's come and gone. Suddenly we were colorful again. That made us both laugh.

First published in 52 | 250 – A Year of Flash

Darryl Price
The Fan (2021)

She left a soft shoe on the floor by the bed that looked like washed out roadkill. Its head was smashed to a flatness that matched its disappearing tail. The once paisley pattern circling the top part resembled a scrunched skeleton hardly held together by dried pink guts. It made me think of her toes. It made me think of her laugh. She wore those shoes like a weapon of choice. She could slip them on and off in a flat second. I could always hear her coming. She wore them at parties. And on movie night. And, finally, she left one behind in her newfound hurry to pack up her few things and jump into his waiting car before the shit hit the fan.

Stella Pierides
Dream Island (2011)

Strolling along a track in the river Evros Delta, in Alexandroupolis, on the border between Greece and Turkey, I could see millions of birds feeding. The lagoons, marshes, and lakes provide a heaven for birds seeking milder weather. The terns, warblers, waders, egrets, oystercatchers, shelducks, eagles, pelicans, cormorants have found their Eden.

This spectacle, together with the eerie quiet of the landscape, was my reason for coming here.

My heart fluttered when I heard a sudden splash. Expecting a big bird, I turned slowly. A human arm momentarily caught in a reed bed, showed out of the water. The flow of the river pushed it past the reeds, sweeping it along on its journey.

I froze. Here, in this idyllic, serene waterland, there is neither space nor tolerance for those fleeing poverty and war. I'd read that on this border alone, hundreds of aspiring immigrants lose their lives every year.

Easing myself on a stone, I remembered my grandmother's story.

When I asked her what happened to those trying to cross Evros escaping the aftermath of the 1922 war between Greece and Turkey, she said that in the middle of the river, there is Dream Island. Lapped by gentle waters, protected by olive, lemon, and fig trees, and warmed by a kind sun, it welcomes those seeking refuge.

Run by angels, who pick up the drowned and the suicides floating past, it is the real heaven on Earth. The birds on the lagoon are their souls.

First published in 52 | 250 – A Year of Flash

Stella Pierides
Story's End (2020)

The body of Scheherazade, a dear friend of mine, was never found, though some say it had been spotted floating in the Thames.

The event did not attract the attention of the media. After all, somewhere along the 213 miles of the Thames, a dead body is washed ashore once a week. Only rarely do these discoveries make the news; the forgotten victims become stories of the river.

Life hadn't been easy for Scheherazade. Long-term unemployment, debts, disease, had plagued my friend for a long time. And now the local council, unaware of her Parkinson's, the extent of which she so carefully kept hidden, evicted her. On her last call to me, she said that however much she tried she couldn't see a way out … her body had been folding upon itself, her heart had been turning to stone. Every evening, fighting painful cramps and insomnia, she relieved her distress by telling herself a story, leaving the ending for the next day, throwing herself a lifeline of hope.

Recently, even this had changed. "I am losing interest in my own stories," she said.

At the time of her disappearance, Scheherazade had been seen walking along the Thames Path.

When I retraced her steps, I was told strangers had been following her to hear the tales that poured out of her mouth. Some had been reduced to tears, it was claimed.

It was as if the stories that had been soothing and life-saving, were now bursting open the gates to the pain of this world.

darkness falls
setting sail on the river's
silent waters

Alex Reece Abbott
Antipodean Pepper Tree
(2010)

I'm right here writing, looking out on the storm-battered roses, but in my head I'm twelve thousand miles south, climbing that giant pepper tree, *Schinus molle*.

Six years old in our back garden in New Zealand, I prune my grandiose tree-house ambitions and settle for a shelf. Two strong flexing branches carry me, chafing rough bark oozing minty, head-clearing milk-sap.

Outside, the rose-petals rain on the wet concrete, but in my mind, I'm still incognito behind that drooping green leaf curtain, still swaying in that warm breeze, still watching the world in peace, right there writing, twelve thousand miles south.

First published by the Arvon Foundation Prize

Alex Reece Abbott
Antipodean Case Moth
(2020)

This morning a photo from Taree flashed on my phone, and my friend Maureen's cocooned case moth sent me flying south again. Twelve thousand miles, to New Zealand. Six years old, in my back garden, observing the world from my pepper tree lair.

The tree where I discovered a perfect cicada husk, a fragile sepia treasure still clinging to the rough bark long after the owner had taken flight.

Schinus molle, where I spied the case moth larva, suspended from a branch—at first glance, a drying bud. Snug in her faun cocoon, her journeys elegantly woven, written in fragments of twigs and leaves that she'd harvested along the way.

Metura elongatus. I watched her extend her armoured thorax from her papoose to weave a silken ladder, watched her dragging her home behind her, climbing, climbing, taking her camouflage where she could find it. Curiosity drew me too close and she retreated, then sealed her case until the danger passed. I watched, waited for her metamorphosis and flight. Now I know, the wingless female never leaves her larval case.

A few years ago, I made a pilgrimage back to my leafy haven. While I'd been away, the new owner had subdivided our quarter-acre and felled my giant pepper tree for the convenience of a smooth concrete driveway. I left, taking my vivid milk-sap memories with me, strong-rooted yet shaken by that long tombstone slab.

Len Kuntz
Rich (2011)

Rimming the volcano of garbage are vultures—fifty or more, their black plumage inky in the smoldering sun. Big as toddlers, they cock their crocked necks as if they know my thoughts, but they do not, no one does.

Last week my son fought one of these evil birds. Marco had discovered an uneaten sandwich in the heap when the creature swooped down.

Thank God Marco had the bent-up umbrella he always carries, sometimes using it as a bat ("Look, Papa, I'm A Rod!"), a dancing cane, ("I'm smooth like your favorite, Gene Kelly!"), a golf club ("Now I'm Chi Chi Rodriguez. How do you like those apples, Papa?") I watched him beat the bird, heard their tangled screaming. We were in the middle of sorting recyclables from other's people's discarded waste. My wife implored me to intervene, but I knew that would only make Marco soft, and soft does not survive here.

We used to live inside the dump, among the maggots and rats, until the missionaries came. Now we have rows of tin boxes to make our homes. Still, a narrow, dirt road is all that separates our make-shift town from the dump.

Miles below sits Puerto Vallarta. At night, she shimmers, a bejeweled gown. A cruise ship glows with its windows white as American teeth.

When I was young like Marco, I often plotted an escape. Now that I am wiser, I watch my family sleeping and feel embarrassed to be this rich.

First published in 52 | 250 – A Year of Flash

Len Kuntz

Shadowboxing (2021)

Midday, but the beach stood nearly deserted. Midday, the sun shooting skeins of light, though the air seemed leaden to Marco, weighing him down the way the sickness had crushed everyone all year. His mother first to go, his father next, his *abuela* somehow still holding on, in their tin shanty, worlds away from the tourist zone.

He trudged through sand, a wooden staff behind his neck, stretched across his shoulders, necklaces of every length and thickness draped down like shiny salamanders, some clattering as Marco approached the grand hotel that faced the ocean.

If security was out, Marco would have to keep walking, but there were none now and so Marco moved in closer.

Poolside, the waiters looked like hospital workers, dressed in cream pants and shirts, all wearing cream face-coverings. The pool itself was flush with tourists, none wearing masks, all stripped down to bathing suits, seemingly unconcerned about the plague that had ravaged the entire world. Marco tried to kill the feeling rising up in his chest, a sensation far stronger than love, something Marco's father had branded a disgusting sin ... *Envy*. So often, it shadowboxed him into contempt and dust.

A lounging blond girl with gleaming skin waved. Marco looked over both his shoulders before realizing she meant him.

When he waved back, she curled her finger in a *Come-here* motion. He didn't know what to do with that, so he copied her gesture, *Come-here*, and to his horror and delight, she did.

Mary Jane Holmes
Set a Crow to
Catch a Crow (2014)

It is the sound that draws her, a tapping on the window like culled wind chimes. She sets aside the plastic-paned envelopes and pushes at the door, blinking through the sunlight. A man stands at the gate freeing rowan suckers from the hinge bound post, a cage of birds at his feet. Their claws skitter against the mesh.

"I've no need for decoys," she says, kicking at the spent ragwort, releasing a seethe of blow-balls across the field. "Bailiffs took the yearlings. Crows' beaks can do little harm now."

The man picks the downy clocks from the air and cracks them between his teeth.

"Good pasture," he says looking over the field thistle, the empty lambing shed, the curve of the brow to the coppice and beck. "Mashams would do well here."

"Debt's the only thing that does well here." She raps the cage with her boot. The crows skirr, the fingered edges of their wings bending against the bars. "And bankruptcy notices won't sire new stock."

She springs the trap, upturning it, and the birds thrash and stab.

The man retrieves the cage. "I've a pair of hill ewes that produce and finish well," he says, turning towards the lane. The woman watches the crows flutter and calm in his arms.

"Need more than ewes."

The man smiles, the gate snapping shut behind him. When he's gone, she leans against it, fingers bent against the bars, watching him as he starts up the hill, trailing his crook behind him.

First published in The Journal of Compressed Creative Arts

Mary Jane Holmes
Vigil (2021)

It is the silence that wakes her, its echo a clock whose pendulum has stilled. She sets aside the drenching syringe and colostrum bundled in her lap and reaches for the crate by the hearth, slips her hand beneath the blankets until she touches the thinly fleeced skin of the lamb. She knows its texture, her Jack felt the same when she found him rigwelted by the new gate to the coppice and beck, a rafter of crows scything the fencing above him.

The hospital room smelt of the dip pens, the sound of his heart, slow like the call of the plover just before rain. Four days now and no sign of waking. After two, they'd sent her home with the promise to call if there was any change; she eyes the telephone as she would a ewe about to labour. She'd never bargained, not at any auction, not when the farm went near to bankruptcy, not when Jack wanted to make an *honest* woman of her, but she would now: this singleton for his life or … she bleezes the fire's embers. The flames birth and she takes the wee thing between her palms and rubs. Nothing. Then the telephone rings and a mewl chords from the throat of the lamb. She swaddles the phone's receiver to her ear as if it were a new-born and feels the tightening around the escapement of her heart.

Tom O'Brien
Thirty Miles from Shore
(2016)

Thirty miles from shore there's only horizon. That's the last thing she told me.

On a skiff, with no strength to row home, I realised her truth was a lie.

The gull who followed me stood on a pillar of air, then waved me to my fate. Flew to a speck. All horizon, no perspective.

This was no place to give up.

I took my cracked oar and pushed the sea behind me once, once more, once more again.

Tom O'Brien
No More Sea (2021)

She wasn't here when I returned but I keep rowing; on a machine in a glass tower, high above the city, high above the sea.

I search but there's no horizon, just seeded clouds, saving us and blinding us.

She sleeps inland now, while I count concrete seasons. No grass grows in spring, no summer hay sways amongst the steel, the autumn tar remains unploughed and no winter livestock comes to us, not for shelter or not for comfort.

Rare days a gull emerges, hoping for unpoisoned land. Wheels away with an unheard call.

At night, when the engines stop, I hear the sea and row in the dark glass to my reflection, where once there was horizon.

Nuala O'Connor
Vincent in the Yellow House (2011)

If I live in a crepuscular haze, he lives in the light. Funny, then, that I choose yellow—sun and butter, spring flowers and madness—and Gauguin revels in devilish reds.

Absinthe swirls my brain toward anger; I eye him.

"Why," I say, "did you put your own features on a painting of me?"

Gauguin frowns. "Because all pictures are portraits of their makers."

I fling my absinthe—glass and all—at his head. He manhandles me from Café de la Gare, across the square to our yellow house.

"Bed," he commands. Sleep muffles me at once.

"I apologise," is my morning greeting, but I continue to watch him.

He steps back from his easel. "I'm going for a walk."

I follow, a razor tucked palm-wise. On the Place Lamartine he turns to me and I plunge the air with the blade. Gauguin runs and I feel remorse; he is my friend.

I return to the house, where my squat, motherly portrait of the Virgin mocks me, screams to my loneliness. Like some biblical traitor, I take my razor and carve a slitch off my ear. I watch the seep of blood mingle with the yellow paint on my palette.

Then I wrap the ear-slice in newspaper, like a rasher of bacon, and take it to Rachel the street-walker. She is not pleased.

Gauguin leaves our house after that and I retreat to the asylum. Safe from the Virgin, safe from the prostitute, safe from Gauguin, safe from yellow.

First published in KYSO Flash

Nuala O'Connor
Nine at the Café Volpini
(2021)

The Café Volpini's waitress pulls out the chair opposite mine and, uninvited, she sits and stares at me.

"Madame," I say, "I wish to swallow my coffee in peace."

"*Un, deux, trois,*" she says, stabbing her fingers around our exhibition of paintings, "*quatre, cinq, six, sept, huit, neuf.*"

"*Brava*, you count as well as any toddler."

She holds my gaze. "Nine male artists, Monsieur Gauguin. Aren't there females who paint? Or are you a disrespecter of women?"

My first thought is, *Oh Lord, save me from quarrelsome shrews.*

My second is this: I pull art from nature while dreaming before it, just as surely as I was pulled from my mother's body, that woman who sewed until her fingers bled to buy me an education. And my darling Mette bore our five beauties, and later taught French to her fellow Danes, to keep wolf after wolf far from us, while I daubed, dipped, and dallied over art—my precious paintings—and travelled away and away, abandoning her finally, all of them, so that my daughter and my four fine sons shy from me, for I am nothing but a stranger to them.

I want to say to this waitress, this extraordinary person, *You are stronger, nobler, more able than I, as is every woman I know. I have been served by you, and by all women, and I sit before you, nothing but a thoughtless wretch.*

Instead, I mutter, "*Mea culpa*, Madame," take to my feet, and hurry away.

Piet Nieuwland

For All the Light
That Was Born (2011)

for all the light that was born in your eyes
this page opens
on it falls the anti-cyclonic day,
and a night sky of silky blues
on it falls the vision of a platinum moon,
its blazing stare swallowing paths of moving shadows
in the ocean upon which it swims,
waves of a tropical artery flower splashes of marlin
in the passage of these islands through their naming,
the language of fire sings from the ridges, the pa
crossing our voices,
a silicon bird surfs the magnetic fields of cool, still air,
tasting seeds of wind
from the silence of stars,
an armada of glass palaces fuse,
into a cathedral of whispering eyes
and the space we occupy fills,
with a rosary of vines

First published in 52|250 – A Year of Flash

Piet Nieuwland
Up There (2021)

After that not much happened. You went away, south I think. The weather became much warmer, the skies hazy and red from the Australian forest fires. Marama, the moon, still rises in the same places and crosses the sky much as it had always done. Some celebrated humans landing there. I remain obsessed by its passage and shades of blues, greys and oranges. Saskia wears t-shirts with phases of the moon. Her doll is named Lunar and there is still a big rabbit up there with long ears—maybe it's a hare now, certainly a here and now. Sometimes Marama becomes a camembert or a brie moon when we buy big round slabs of cheese at a discount store where items are near their use by date. At Matariki we celebrate with a pavlova moon, it seems appropriate somehow. I doubt the moon will ever be any or either of them, edible, but we enjoy pretending it is.

The ocean is warmer than ever. I watch it from a distance almost every day, from this hill-top. It's more the winds that occupy me now. And the clouds, the thoughts of clouds, the noctilucents super high in the mesosphere, responding to methane from pastures way down here. At school I was the nephologist, giving the cloud report each morning. You listened while knitting. The threads of time stretch and weave. Pull a knot here and look what happens, we appear before each other in the haze.

T M Upchurch
Sand (2010)

He bounced over the beach, twirling and leaping as sunlight warmed the breeze on his belly, like when he and Janie were six. His jacket slid down his arms into a Batman cape and he laughed, skidding to a stop and crashing onto his back, mouth open and eyes wide.

"In't they lovely …"

A voice made him jump. He twisted to see two women tucked beneath the dunes, soaking up the sight of three tiny sisters stampeding sandcastles.

"Aw, dumplin's …"

Caramel puddings sticky with salt, the youngest looked past her mother right into his eyes so he beamed and mouthed, "Janey?"

She beamed back.

"Carrie! Here." Woman, leaping up with sand running in rivulets over her frock. Glaring at the man with the scar who grinned at little girls. Herding her daughters in a furious flap. Frosty silence until his smile faded and he stood, backed away, tried to go forward, backed away again, hypnotised by the pulse of forwards, backwards, forwards so that he carried on rocking even as the mother bustled her brood away.

Murmurs, "… off his head."

He watched them go. Woman and small girl out of reach. Like the day the truck took Mum and Janie. Leaving him to dance a child's step all alone, heal the hole in his head, try to move forward, back, forward, back, never understanding the stares nor why his fingers could not keep hold of sand.

First published in 52|250 – A Year of Flash

T M Upchurch
Seams (2021)

My fingers trace the dimples and ridges of his forehead and shiny knots of his cheeks, to the deep crease, almost a slash, around his lips. I feel his waking breath, almost at peace. I can still touch his scars without him flinching, the only remaining sign of our seamlessness.

I feel him. I feel his morning stretch, his chew and swallow, his peering out of the window to see the weather. I feel the sun on his forehead, the rain trickling down his neck, the tightness of his calves and the burn in his feet, as he hikes, day after day, to look for me.

I'm here, Joey. Here, I used to say.

He'd stare, anger flaring. *I'm not looking for you, I'm looking for Janey.*

He doesn't hear. His body can't take me in, his brain forever scrambled, his nerves forever torn. He can only remember the little girl whose movements matched his own, from long before birth.

He goes with a rocking, dancing gait, head swinging from side to side. Searching for Janey.

I drink coffee, read the papers, make calls and laugh with friends—but when he leaves, my body twists and my legs feel the dance. My eyes search for a little girl that even I can't see any more.

I'll follow, until we find her again.

John Wentworth Chapin
Double Vision (2010)

Angela knew the sensation she caused as she neared Jeanne's casket carrying a white rose; it would agonize everyone at the gravesite to watch the identical twin approach. The girls had always been together, from moments after conception and first meiosis till 28 years later when the elevator decapitated Jeanne as she struggled to extricate herself from the doors, Angela at her side. Now the survivor faced the perished, those two identical faces brought together one last time. She knew the increased weeping from the folding chairs on the grass was as much for her, remaining in the world alone without her constant companion, as it was for Jeanne—always one life, one identity, one half. To conceive of them separated was unthinkable to every wet-eyed soul at the burial.

Angela imagined tomorrow: free for the first time. Neither had ever dared let the other out of her sight from overwhelming horror that one might secure an advantage, might get something that the other didn't have. She dropped the rose on the polished cherrywood and prayed for there to be no God, for the stories to be just that: stories. The possibility that Jeanne had an afterlife refueled in Angela's heart the furious hatred that had burned there bright for twenty-eight years.

First published in 52|250 – A Year of Flash

John Wentworth Chapin
Rope (2021)

Then

Seven years old: overwhelming rage. The girls fight, so Jeanne barricades herself in their bedroom. The door kicks open from the father's shoe at shoulder height, screws ripped from the door frame. He snatches her roughly, tears at underwear and elastic flowered pants, slaps her bare flesh with callused hands.

She feels anger, then pain, then the aftershock of that pain crest over her twin. A tremor quakes along the tie that binds them. *NO!* screams Angela from the hall. *Punish me, too!* Their father does not understand. Jeanne smirks at her sister as the blows rain down on her flesh.

Now

She feels Angela, the cord unseverable even in death. When Angela thinks of her dead sister, the cord quivers. A chill passes through Jeanne, but the dead feel nothing. It is her sister's own living terror.

An opportunity ripens: Jeanne senses the connection go taut. She wiggles it, carefully reeling a fish, testing the strength of the line and waiting for the moment to pull.

BETWEEN DRUMBEATS

Jane Hammons
Before Leaving Town (2010)

Between drumbeats and steel guitar rhythms, I break up with your brother. Like sisters, you and I dance a mean Cotton-Eyed Joe.

First published in 52 | 250 – A Year of Flash

Jane Hammons
While We Danced (2021)

Three men convicted of horrific crimes escaped from jail and later
that night murdered your brother. In dawn that followed, I left,
drove back to college.

I returned for the funeral and other occasions: your wedding;
mine
and then less
and
less
often
until
I was
gone
and you
let
go

Until
thirty-five years pass
we talk
again
divorced children grown you grandchildren

We edge our way back
to friendship
its seal broken
murdered
it crept away
lacking words
the ability to understand
the ineffable
not meant to be understood we understand
now.

Together
we return to the cemetery
hometown
distant
now
to us
but forever
his.

I had forgotten his middle name was Sidney.

Like sisters, you and I dance a mean Cotton-Eyed Joe.

Rachel Smith
Night Shadows (2014)

There weren't many out tonight, just his gang working on the wet road.

Nathan turned his back to the rain and pulled out one of the cigarettes he'd carefully rolled hours earlier.

The paper soaked up drops of water from his hand, and even hunched over out of the wind it was hard to light. He pulled hard until the end began to glow brightly and he could feel the warm smoke running down and through him.

Lights from a car played past and an old car pulled up alongside him. Nathan turned to look, tucking his cigarette behind the shelter of his body.

Her long dark hair was pulled back; impatient fingers played out a tune on the steering wheel. She should have been home in bed not driving through dark streets with the doors unlocked.

He reached out a hand, close enough to touch the car if he leaned just a little, his body hidden in night shadows.

Her mouth opened and she began to sing, tilting the mirror to watch herself—eyes narrowed, lips pouted and body moving against the seat.

The door handle felt cool under his hand.

Her shoulders moved from side to side, and her head swung heavily towards him.

For a stinging second their eyes met.

The light turned green and a horn tooted.

She gathered her face together, flicked him the finger and put her foot down.

Nathan leaned casually back, lifted his cigarette to his mouth, and took a drag.

First published in Flash Frontier: An Adventure in Short Fiction

Rachel Smith
The Kiss (2021)

We sit in the front seat. He stops the car outside my house, keeps it running.

Sophia has told me the basics. Open your mouth a little. Let him put his tongue in. Don't do it first. Close your eyes—his face will look weird up that close. She and I practiced on damp pillows, our own reddened arms. Once on each other, breathless at our bravery.

I take off my seatbelt, wait, hear the click–slide as he does the same.

I know the tilted heads and slickly matched lips from the movies. I know my brother and his girlfriend, the snake thrust of his tongue into her mouth, the push of his groin.

He reaches an arm out, turns the music up. The radio fills the car with noise. I can feel and not hear my heart escaping.

At the movies, I did not eat popcorn in case a kernel stuck in my teeth. I drank water and not Coke in case the sugar coated my tongue. I chewed a piece of gum 20 times when I went to the toilet before we left.

I look his way and he is so close that I can see the pin–dot-white of a spot on his chin. I close my eyes.

The next day I ring Sophia. I tell her it was warm and wet, that our teeth banged five times and his breath smelt of onions. I tell her that I think I am in love.

Michelle McEwen
Miss Lamb's Love Advice
(2010)

Don't worry about love—that's what Miss Lamb says whenever her niece comes over weeping and wailing about some man. Miss Lamb is sixty-something and she's through with love. Whenever she hears a woman talking about looking for love, her favorite thing to say is: "You looking for love? Why? I ain't. All I want is a good night's sleep." Then she laughs and says, "Watch, once you get old like me, you don't wanna be bothered." Miss Lamb was engaged once, but the man tried to boss her around. That engagement lasted a year; she knew then marriage wasn't for her. "I see it like this," she once said, "the only women meant to be wives are fool-women."

Yesterday, I was sitting in Miss Lamb's kitchen—crying and carrying on (though this wasn't my intention) about some good love gone bad. Miss Lamb rolled her eyes in her what-I-tell-you-'bout-love way. She said, turning on her oven for heat, "I don't deal with love, but one thing I know 'bout love is really good love don't go bad." My tears stopped then. She took my hand, said: "You know when you got a good dress that fit you well? It's tight in the right spots and no matter how much you wear or wash it, it stays fittin you the same. Well, a bad made dress will loosen up after a few washes—now that was a no-good dress from the start." Miss Lamb knows what she's talking about.

First published in 52 | 250 – A Year of Flash

Michelle McEwen
Miss Lamb's Love Language (2021)

Miss Lamb. Oh, Miss Lamb. Miss 'don't-worry-about-love' Lamb. Miss 'once-you-get-to-my-age-you-don't-wanna-be-bothered' Lamb. I remember when it used to be that Miss Lamb (with her two fat black cats and her ten kinds of black tea) would sit back and talk so bad about love you'd think love skipped town with some money it owed her. Today, though, Miss who-needs-love Lamb came over with a smile on her mouth and in her eyes. "You seen that article in yesterday's paper about love language," she asked. She looked taller, leaner. She said, "You know my youngest niece wrote that!" She said, "You know I don't go for all this love stuff but as for this love language stuff, I think mine would be quality time."

James Claffey
Bingo Night (2011)

Laundry detergent, bread, cauliflower, nasal spray, deodorant, chili pepper flakes, condoms, half-a-dozen size AAA eggs, crème fraîche, 60-watt light bulbs, *People* magazine, a DVD of *The Quick and the Dead*, and a shower hat. Linda totes her basket on one arm, the mobile phone cradled against her ear, whilst the other hand scratches beneath the underwire of her brassiere. Her skin is broken, veined and blue, and she itches like fucking crazy. Tonight she visits her brother-in-law, while her sister, Mavis, goes to Bingo in the Parish Hall. Linda can't understand why her sister bothers to go to Bingo. Mavis once confided, "The thought of shouting 'BINGO' in front of everyone makes me sick to my stomach." Yet for fourteen years she's played the game every Wednesday night, and for every one of those fourteen years of Wednesday nights, Linda has secretly been fucking her sister's husband, Eduardo, who has been fucking her in the laundry room, Linda's bare ass-cheeks visible in the dust on the dryer lid. He likes to crack the eggs on her ass, and then dip celery, peppers, and cauliflower between her legs. After their lovemaking he makes a frittata while Linda removes her toenail polish and repaints her stubby toes with a fresh coat. For fourteen years she's only used Mavis's varnish. "Two fat ladies, eighty-eight." Linda forks a mouthful of cauliflower and egg into her mouth and smiles at Eduardo. "Bingo, Bingo, Bingo."

First published in Up the Staircase

James Claffey
Metempsychosis (2021)

The surgeon's hands tanned and hairless. *Perhaps he shaves them?* I think, as he pulls on the latex gloves and calls for his scalpel. The shine dazzles. As he carves into puckered flesh it feels like the cold of the washing machine on those long-ago Wednesdays. A reflection in the steel; eyes too dark, bags beneath them, hair as gray and wiry as a badger's pelt. I hold my breath as the surgeon exposes my heart. A papery object filled with boxes and numbers, it flutters, and the surgeon raises both hands in supplication. "Heaven's Gate, eighty-eight," he calls. I peer from behind and blow a hot breath towards my still heart in his smooth hands. Across my chest a tapestry of wires deconstructed as the chipped nail varnish of my yellowed toenails fades.

The title is taken from the Greek *meta* (after) and *empsychos* (to animate) – from *en-* + psyche (soul).

Bob Eckstein

Broke Up with My Hairdresser (2010)

It wasn't that he dropped the comb on the floor and just continued using it or that I was bleeding behind my neck from a nick. No, the last straw came when I saw him in the mirror wipe his running nose with a bare hand which he then dipped into hair gel before running his hands through my head. I didn't say anything, too stunned and mortified. Just went home and took two showers. What do you tip something like that?

First published in 52 | 250 – A Year of Flash

Bob Eckstein
Hairdresser (2021)

First published in Weekly Humorist

David Eggleton
Big City Rush Hour (1986)

Cloud pops out,
a body-builder posing.
Heat grills each car on the grid,
bronze light slashes off the windows.
A bus sways forward concertina-style.
A finance house stacks up its cool vertical lines,
calculator-thin.
This town stands as open as an airport lounge.
Everyone looks like a new arrival.

First published in South Pacific Sunrise
(Penguin Books NZ, 1986)

David Eggleton
Autogeddon (2022)

Horn cadences cascade; storied car parks climb. On the spaghetti western motorway, thoroughbreds gallop, nags limp, and tall trucks wobble like prairie wagons.

Nearing traffic cone country, highways clot to snail pace. The hi-viz vest squad in earmuffs weed-whacks a berm. Beeping to get a wriggle on, stuck in crawlspace, a driver chews her bubble-gum to boiling point.

Bull-bars bunt like antlers; paddle-pops guard zebra crossings; cat's eyes blink; skateboarders bumper-hang; tyre-tread signs the dotted line. The tailback jam's a slow-moving glacier, compounded of frozen glances and tiny fists beating against insides of windscreens.

Past the bottleneck, traffic swarms as one, like wasps from a nest knocked out of a tree. Motorbike throttles open up on the scenic route. Mag wheels revolve quickly over slick tar-seal, but pause delicately for the breath-testing queue.

Out of the dark heart of night cars transform, with flashing grilles and sleeved headlamps and aerodynamic stripes, to samurai warriors, to the judder of kabuki theatre, to racer circuits between stoplights. Truckies ratchet up the ante and gun their big rigs; possums are mashed into pizza topping.

End of the road is Autogeddon's scrapheap: confiscated, crushed, melted for road-signs.

Randal Houle
Speedy the Slug (2010)

On the news, the economy is all bad, but you'd never know it from my viewpoint washing dishes at Chan's Open Kitchen. Just like that Charles Dickens thing on TV. "Stuff's kinda good. Stuff's also kinda bad."

You can't see me. I'm all the way in the back drying clean dishes with a filthy rag. My roommate, Quon, waited tables and fed me information about the patrons. After work, we'd get so high that we'd slip off the couch onto the floor and cuddle while the record player crackled and cadenced until one of us realized the needle never reset and we would fall asleep.

"See that guy." Quon pointed and I searched through a small portal. A man in November courted May. She laughed and pawed at his shoulder. "That rich bastard's got it all, poor guy."

Just then, the woman's mouth dropped. She grabbed her Martini and threw it. The man's head was drenched. Quon said it was a dry Martini and I howled. I bolted out the back door to the alley and laughed my ass off and that's when I saw it—a slug racing away, leaving a trail of shiny muck in its wake.

First published in 52|250 – A Year of Flash

Randal Houle
Thank You for Stopping By (2020)

Ten years later, the news says the economy is all good. Maybe it is. How would I know? You might remember I followed a slug down an alley. That's how I lost my job at Chan's Open Kitchen. Something about job abandonment. I didn't know the job needed me more than I needed it. Live and learn.

You can't see me, doing dishes in my university apartment kitchen during quarantine. My old roommate and best friend Quon passed away nine years ago. I know, I'm sorry for your loss and thank you for saying that. I'm afraid the old record player is gone, too. Had to hock it for cash. But some evenings, I close my eyes and pretend Quon is here. I wrap my arms around myself and imagine us holding each other. Sometimes I even hear the crackle and pop from the old record player. Sometimes that makes me smile. Sometimes that makes me incredibly sad and I slide down the front of the couch and cry.

When it rains, a small puddle forms outside the back door. A seal on the threshold keeps the water from leaking in, but if you open it, earthworms wriggle from the bottom part of the door which actually carries them inside where they drop onto the linoleum and wriggle around like only worms can.

Derek Ivan Webster
Rash Decision (2011)

She made that face when he said it, the one that reminded him of his mother. He took a deep breath and tried to keep his tone even. What came out was script swiped straight from the old man.

"Who in their right mind wants to come home to this!" he bellowed.

She watched him from the couch. The baby was nursing on her lap; the fullness of her breast burst free of her shirt and smothered the sleeping pinkness. He could remember when such softness was meant for him: her warm weight pressed against his face. She had not touched him since the hospital.

"Got it out of your system?" He didn't respond. "Good, then you can change the diaper." She held the wrinkly bundle out. The baby looked peaceful wrapped so tightly in its blanket. He knew exactly how long that would last.

The little body writhed, its screams rattling the changing table. The pad was already drenched with piss. There was a violent looking rash between the legs. The warmer stood empty and overturned to the side, the last wet-one used. Another deep breath as he watched his baby wail against the world.

A hand touched him on the shoulder. He felt the fingertips reach past his collar and trace the skin of his neck.

"We need you, you know," she said.

He knew. He opened his hand and she gave him a wipe.

"She's beautiful," he nodded, and decided to let the rash air itself out.

First published in 52 | 250 – A Year of Flash

Derek Ivan Webster
Kerfuffle (2021)

She was taller than him by a breath. She wore flats around the house and stooped, just enough, whenever they were in the same room.

"Curfew?" He held her by the bare shoulders, just above the powder blue ruffle of her dress.

"Midnight." She held her face neutral.

"We agreed on eleven."

"We agreed that you trust me."

He shook his head. "Don't slouch."

She straightened up, raised her chin; their eyes met, level. He looked old, and not just around the eyes. The neck she'd once swung from had shriveled and bent.

She glanced down at her phone. "My ride's here."

"He couldn't come in?"

"We're already late."

She stepped back and gave a wave with her fingertips. His arms stayed outstretched. "Wait." The plea caught her step, almost enough to make her turn.

"Boys ..."

"Yeah?"

"They're no good. No matter what they say, you can't trust them."

They were both looking at her hands now, the phone she held. A muffled scraping came from upstairs: boxes being moved around. The phone pinged.

She let her breath out. "I trust *you.*"

The phone pinged again. It took a moment for the tiny sound to fade.

"Okay."

"Okay?"

"Your mom and I will be waiting. At midnight."

She left the house, the creak of her father behind her, making his shuffling way upstairs.

Nod Ghosh
Coloured Hands (2001)

The woman's hands were painted yellow and red. She wove between stationary cars, howling, showing her coloured palms to anyone who'd look.

The lights changed and I inched forward, drove away from the woman, away from the building with *Call to Islam* written on the side, away from a man carrying a bucket. The bucket looked heavy.

I'd argued with Ted; couldn't remember how the quarrel had started. Throwing some crocosmia corms into a bag, I left without a goodbye. I'd dug the nuggets up weeks ago. Eleanor had asked for them, and I should've taken them to her. They'd sat in the sun, and I wasn't sure if they'd survive. I didn't care. I wasn't sure of our friendship anymore. I wasn't sure about much.

Eleanor opened the door, hands deep in pockets. We drank tea outdoors under the shade of an acacia.

"What's in the bag?" she asked.

"Crocosmia corms."

"Why?"

"You wanted some," I said.

"Oh yes."

"Also known as monbretia or copper tips." I pulled one from the bag. "They're originally from South Africa."

"You know a lot about them."

"I like the orange flowers. I like all orange flowers."

"I remember." Eleanor wiped the underside of her mug with her sleeve.

"I'm leaving Ted." My voice cracked with the truth of it.

Eleanor's eyes moistened, as if she'd known, but was waiting to be told.

I sought out the woman with painted hands on my way home, but she wasn't there anymore.

First published with the Leeds People's Writing Group

Nod Ghosh
Orange Flowers (2021)

Someone sends orange flowers for my birthday: gerberas, marigolds, and zinnias. Wisps of crocosmia protrude from the yellow-red dome. Taking them from the deliveryman's callused hands, my *thank-you* is effusive, as if the man himself has presented me with the bouquet.

The card is decorated with orange blooms too.

Remembering you on your special day, T-bear. I'd stopped using Ted's pet name once divorce loomed. He's never given me flowers before, so his gesture seems irrelevant now, nonsensical even. I don't have a large enough vase, so I place the bunch in a bucket. Making tea, I wipe emotion away with milk splashes and sugar.

Perhaps I should thank Ted, but it can wait.

Later, I sculpt my response.

Thanks.

Too stark. Erase.

Cheers for the gift.

Sprightly. Still not right.

I wish things hadn't ended the way they did.

No, that won't do.

Thank you for the flowers.

Too polite. I don't feel polite.

Can flowers undo the damage you did?

No. Don't show him I'm broken.

Bastard.

Don't give him the satisfaction of a curse-word.

Orange is at odds with my melancholic mood. You could have sent blue.

Absolutely not. This is Eleanor's work. She'll have reminded him I like orange flowers. Ted doesn't remember details. Not like I do.

I saw a man with callused hands today. He reminded me of you.

To hint at his callous indifference? Doesn't seem right. Nothing is right.

Because how can anything be right, when everything is so wrong?

Iona Winter
Lost Marbles (2015)

My grandfather sleeps a lot these days. When he's awake he repeats the same questions, or remembers random facts from the past.

"I owned a Chevrolet Impala in 1967."

Way before my time.

He lost his marbles, searching for words that had always been abundant in forthcoming.

Then my grandmother started speaking more often, through him, but with her own words. She was like a mind reader.

"He wants to gather shellfish," she said one afternoon.

This thing needed no words. And so, we went.

Our toes dug at the water's edge, searching for hardness beneath the sand. Dinner.

He thought I was my mother. I didn't correct him.

An incoming wave swished through our woven basket of molluscs, splashing his rolled-up trousers. Granddad looked at me and laughed.

"I know what you're up to," he said with a wink.
"She wanted me out of the house."

First published at Ad Hoc Fiction

Iona Winter

Madwoman (2022)

I've been silenced for lifetimes, and these days some say I'm too visible in my pain.

Often, I find myself lingering by children's shoes in shops, remembering. And I sit in the corner at meetings, to make myself invisible, head down, listening as mothers talk about their children, when mine is no more.

They say a mad woman lives next door.

Sometimes at night I am dragged from sleep, to listen to her ranting outside to darkened tree shadows and those she communes with beneath them.

I reckon people are afraid of her but she doesn't seem a threat to me, despite her loud exclamations and the slamming of doors.

I admire her ability to let it out, whereas my thoughts remain closed inside like a hardened nut long past its use-by date. There is both majesty and magic in her night-time chatter, above the constant hum of the port.

Robert Vaughan
No More I Love Yous
(2011)

For someone who's barely
acknowledged me, he now
oozes I love you …
I love you …
so much that I
disappear.
I liked it better
before, left up
to me. When I had
no clue. I found
peace in that
silent forest.
Fascination.

First published in 52 | 250 – A Year of Flash

Robert Vaughan
Four Myths (2021)

^Myth One^

Against the fog he was a big man. Against the fire tower he stood out like Paul Bunyan. And there were a great many folks who respected him: firefighter, crusader, bowler of the year. Award-winning spelunker. But we're his other family. Who would have even known? Not me, not my sister. I try not to remember. I try to tamp down the stink.

?Myth Two?

Somebody said she did it for kicks. Another said it was all for attention. I thought it was pretty stupid. Christmas Day. Hovering over a fence along a country road? Wearing just a gauzy slip? A surefire way to end up in the loony-bin where Aunt Tina is a lifelong resident. My sister has done some fairly idiotic things, and this was just another in the line of icy dumbass dumb-ness.

{Myth Three}

Let's play marco polo she said. I'm unsure you can do that in the ocean. The roar of the waves, the salt in your ears. The leadbelly bottom and sandy rewards. I said let's disappear into the surf, dissolve into foamy crests, cremate our desires into damp, fertile depths. {hold our breaths forever, in unison}.

/Myth Four\

Another small town filled with cheer. You couldn't miss the liquor sign. Tallest sign in the county, higher than any billboard, larger than every building. Lit up at night, like my daddy was, mostly. Sometimes, the /q\ and the /u\ would flicker off, and the rest of the word, 'lior' reminded me of what I did after he touched me.

Robert Scotellaro
Hit Man in Retirement
(2009)

He awoke and dragged their bodies out of bed. He told himself it was the arthritis. Over coffee the voices were there (the usual suspects) some turning, startled, before a word could be uttered: the spray. Others begging—the big money offers, eyes bugged and jittery. One even offering his wife for a pass and a chance to leave the country.

But a job was a job, and what was a man if he couldn't do what he set out to do, be counted on. He glanced at the newspaper, some headlines, and shook his head with a *what's-the-world-coming-to* lopsided twist to his mouth. He looked forward to checking out the Obits.

There were some pigeons outside on the sill. They sounded like they were in love. He put out a few crumbs, but they fluttered off. They'd soon circle back. When he was younger he would have snapped their necks. He wondered if Janis would call. Thirty-two years apart and he still liked a word or two. All those years she never asked questions.

He slow-walked back to the kitchen—dragged a few bodies with him—their shoes scraping along the linoleum.

First published in 52 | 250 – A Year of Flash

Robert Scotellaro

From a Hit Man's Sketchy Last Will and Testament Written on a Placemat at The House of Pancakes (In Postscript) (2020)

PS

You'll find the key to a safety deposit box in the hollowed out copy of the one Agatha Christie novel in my bookcase. Sorry I cannot disclose how I came upon all that cash but since you are an only child IT'S ALL YOURS. Let's just say it came from "investments" and leave it at that. Too bad your ma isn't still alive. I could have gotten her that house in Jersey she always wanted. Timing can be an asshole. When she had the time, I didn't have the dough. But that's another story.

PPS

Anyways please get rid of any guns you find around the house. I've become very forgetful in old age and have the feeling there are still one or two that need to be discarded. DO NOT KEEP THEM! But my ceramic elephant collection is something you might want. Notice how all the trunks are facing up. That means good luck. You never want them with the trunks facing down. That's bad news. See, you learned something.

PPPS

Okay so everything I did I did and that's that. Now you be a good boy and take all that money and walk the straight and narrow. It's not always easy but the way to go. Trust me on that one. I wish I could have been around more but you were always in my heart. Maybe this will make up for that at least a little. Maybe not, but I'm hoping it will. Enjoy the elephants.

James Norcliffe
Five Travellers in a Small Ford (2015)

Five travellers in a small Ford travelled across the Ardennes. The Hautes Fagnes. The High Fens.

The fifth traveller, strapped in a car seat, cried with hunger.

Clumps of cotton grass rose from the bog land on either side.

The car pulled off the road for the fourth traveller to nurse the fifth traveller.

The sky was grey and despite the late spring there were patches of snow in the shadows.

The third traveller puzzled at his mobile as the navigation system was awry. Luckily, a signpost directed the travellers towards Eupen.

The second traveller, seated beside the third traveller, regretted not making muffins or packing fruit, as like the fifth traveller, the other travellers were hungry.

In 1940 Eupen was declared *judenfrei*. Its citizens celebrated.

The first traveller sat in the shadows of a deserted stadium and put his notebook to one side.

He was a liar.

There was no fifth traveller, no fourth traveller, no third traveller and no second traveller.

This was ok. For this is fiction.

In 1940 there were no Jews in Eupen.

This was not ok.

This was not fiction.

First published in

Landmarks: National Flash Fiction Day UK Anthology

James Norcliffe
Four Travellers in an Austin Maxi (2021)

They sang it in the ming-blue (or brown?) Austin as it climbed over the mountain.

They sang it on the white road through the gloom of the beech forest.

The white dust—the past? or perhaps it was brown—billowed behind.

Sometimes I joined in: *O Veederzane! Sweetheart!*

A strange and haunting name, the promise of an impossible love, like Marlene, like Mercedes under a lamplight in European mist.

One traveller remembers a road littered with handbags, another antlered creatures in the trees, the third recalls the red hot water bottle growing cold, the fourth remembers nothing.

A girl named Goodbye. How many times did I dream of her before I said hello to you?

The sky would know. The blue sky—or perhaps brown—that followed the impossible rain.

Kelly Grotke
All the Peace and Fraternity of the Free World (2011)

It's a true story, I read it in *Life* magazine soon after the war, in between the ads. One was for some new kind of packaging for keeping Mr. Lobster moist and happy all the way from Maine to your table. I suppose I remember that because of the contrast, y'know? All that post-war confidence fizzling up like champagne, champagne and lobsters, that's what the world was going to be and we were going to lead the charge into some bright new future of peace and prosperity. Well, this guy liked lobsters too, he liked all the good things money can buy, and he wasn't middle-class American respectable about it either. Because if you criticized him, he might arrange for a thin loop of wire with a handle on it to be tied around your head. They mentioned that in the article. It's the turning that does it. I mean, they had laws there but this guy's laws were so crazy that you could be put in prison for saying that the summer's there are awful hot. Defamation, see? So yeah, he's heard that someone said a few words against him here or there, and he has the guy picked up and tortured, quite clearly tortured and killed, and afterwards he has the body dropped off to the family, all wrapped up like some bloody entrails in butcher's paper. And then he goes to the house. To comfort the family. It's a true story. You can't make this shit up.

First published in 52 | 250 – A Year of Flash

Kelly Grotke
Nudge (2021)

His confidence increased alongside the prizes and accolades. What had started with a playful, modest series of economic calculations and equations about the conditions under which promises were either kept or broken had become a project of such predictive magnitude that he was now regularly asked to speak on matters of the utmost seriousness. How to end wars and heal social divisions, the meaning of morality, the causes of poverty, whether humans have free will, how to heal a dying planet. Politicians at home and abroad sought out his advice, making him a fixture at the most important global summits.

The public appetite for certainty and reassurance those days was nearly insatiable, and as his reputation grew, so did his wealth. He now had a fine summer home on the coast of Maine, and was able to indulge in the finest restaurants, the rarest wines, the most discerning art. Some might say he'd become rather a caricature, but if so, he was a contented one. He'd earned his place.

Some evenings before bed, he'd think back on how it had all began. He'd think about little Alfred, and that maple tree behind the house in Syracuse. How they'd secretly climbed it together after dinner that day, higher than ever before. He could still see the fear in Alfred's face as they neared the top, the frozen panic, and it fascinated him. Yes, I'd promised to help him get down, he thought. Just not the way he'd expected, poor guy.

Lynn Jenner
Pink Light (2010)

Certain historical figures seem to me to emit pink light. This can take the form of a soft glow with no discernible moment of beginning. It can also be loud and vulgar, accompanied by fairground music, like a pinball machine.

Houdini first began to light up for me when he ended his upside down straight jacket escape with 'Then I am entirely free'. When he hired seven men to sit outside a Left Bank café in Paris, each with one letter painted on his bald head

H O U D I N I noggins
At the Trocadéro

more lights came on.

First published in Dear Sweet Harry
(Auckland University Press, 2010)

Lynn Jenner
For Ever, Harry (2021)

I'm no swimmer but for a couple of years I cast off from solid ground and let myself float in Houdini's pink glow. My chest swelled with his Jewish immigrant ambition. My head swirled with his klezmer music. When he took too long to undo his chains, deep in the Hudson river, my lungs burned. If I'd been there when those college students from Montreal punched Houdini in the belly, I would have wrapped Harry in my arms and called for an ambulance. I would *never* have let him perform the next show.

In 2015 I paid homage at the Diggers Rest monument to Houdini's 1911 flights in his Voisin biplane. Just last week I heard a new Klezmer tune that made me think of his cocky heart-breaking spirit.

Since Houdini there have been affairs of varying lengths with Charles Brasch and Boris Pasternak. At the present time I am hypnotised by a warm white light around a particular house I lived in between 1978 and 1983 and the complicated dust-filled air around the Red Army as it makes its final stand at Stalingrad in 1942. I have always been like this. But until Houdini I did not know how bright that light could be.

Harry Houdini
Zichrono livracha.
May his memory be a blessing.

John Riley
Testimony (2010)

The next winter the house burned down. The summer before
Bobby lived with us. He was short with a thick mustache and big
muscles and didn't like wearing a shirt in the heat. He showed me
how to make a belt snap by looping the end to the buckle and
jerking it from both sides. It's trickier than it sounds when you're
a little kid. You'd catch a finger if you weren't careful and have
to worry about crying. I walked around snapping his belt until
Mom yelled at me to please for God's sake please stop. "I can't
take it anymore," she said. He did card tricks too but wouldn't
show me how they worked. I could figure them out when I grew
up. Now I think about it maybe his name wasn't Bobby. The first
day he wasn't there I kept my mouth shut. The next day I asked
where he'd gone. "Back to the jail he came from," she said.

First published in 52 | 250 – A Year of Flash

John Riley
Building Time (2021)

Nights I slept in a cell, days collected trash along the interstate. My one buddy was Vic Allred who, while drunk, had beat his friend to death with a pool cue. He never told me why. Vic was a model prisoner. I'd sold pot to Deputy Leonard and was no danger to anyone. Vic liked to talk about the books he read and swore he'd never take up religion. We agreed I had no business there. He promised to protect me this go-round but said he would fuck me himself if I ever came back. Not much happened during my eight months. I learned to sleep beneath yellow lights, to not decipher whispers. I helped guys write letters home and read *The Plague,* George Jackson, Dostoevsky, "The Lady with a Little Dog," and whatever else I could scrape up. I believed in dialectical materialism, tried to not think about my release date. I don't remember much more. My girlfriend changed while I was away. College the next year was sweet and wild; I decided to major in the History of Ideas. After five years my record was expunged. One morning years later I read in the newspaper that Vic had escaped and held up a drug store with a stolen gun.

Lola Elvy
Nightfall (2010)

The sun melts
behind purple hills

The moon climbs
on a ladder of hidden stars

A quilt of snow cloaks
the forest floor

Snowdrops glisten
in the bushes

The day's last loon cries
to her young

       And then silence.

An owl hoots
The night awakens

First published in 52 | 250 – A Year of Flash

Lola Elvy
Nightfall II (2021)

He stands over it, earth eking its way between his toes. The
creature looks foreign, not of this world, this sky. Its deathbed
gathers around its body like feathers statically charged, clinging
desperately to the figure's form. The wind is grey.
Rain whispers of birth.

He steps around it, slowly, as if the ground were a living thing:
fragile, and ready to be broken. His feet are heavier now than they
used to be, but when he walks, he feels like a child.
The heart is silent.

All the points that led him here. A lust for life—a longing, even—a
principle. His principle used to be so clear, like that of Archimedes,
a balancing act of natural forces. As indisputable as compass
points: north-south, power-weakness, sink-float.

Does he know nothing about floating?
What is he to learn about sinking?

He looks at the animal, blades of grass rising up like tiny towers
around its jaw. How the mighty fall still. It lies on its side, its
stomach turned to the sky. It looks like it could have dropped from
the heavens themselves. A shadow from the setting sun, a gift.

Nathan Alling Long
Alignment (2011)

They lived in the same neighborhood, biked the same streets, went to potlucks at the same collective houses. What they remember of summer nights is drinking beer on front porches as joints floated through the air like fireflies, kissing each person's lips. Talking of Rilke and Descartes until dawn. Walking home in the rain.

Then autumn came. They pulled out old gray sweaters from their closets. They biked with coats and scarves. Evenings became large bottles of wine and steaming kitchens. Fresh bread from the oven. Everyone sitting on the floor, mismatched plates in their laps, the house dog circling the crowd like a shark, looking for scraps.

One night, near solstice, a few stayed up, improvising an epic poem in rhyme. One by one, they fell asleep, on the sofa, curled up on the rug, against each other's bodies. The candles burned out, the night grew dark.

Then the moon snuck in. It brushed across three faces, the way a moth might glide past your arm. Each woke to the light, and without a word, they began to kiss one another. They had never seen each other in this light before. They kissed and kissed, as the moon trailed across their faces. It was like drinking milk from a distant planet.

Then their portion of the room drew dark, they grew tired, and, with fingers interlocked, they fell asleep. Later, when the moonlight slid across the dog's tail, it awoke and sighed, then fell back asleep.

First published in 52 | 250 – A Year of Flash

Nathan Alling Long
Solstice (2021)

On winter solstice, they planned a long walk in the woods, but got side-tracked, washing dishes, feeding the dog, doing laundry, shopping. When they finally got to the park, dog in tow, it was already dusk.

Still, they walked along the silent, black, shimmering river. Snow from the day before was covered with tracks, but the park now was empty. A half-moon shone through the clouds onto the icy ground, making everything glow below the bare black branches of the trees.

Far along, they met a young man with a husky. The two dogs played, breaking into a slow, silent dance, their forearms up in the air, tapping against each other some ancient, secret animal code. The three watched the dogs play, circling over and over in the snow.

The man reminded the couple of someone they'd known back in college. Gordon. The three had met at a party one night and spontaneously started kissing. They never saw him again, though the couple became lovers and eventually married. Over the years, they never talked of him, though neither one ever forgot him.

And now here was this look-alike man, his dog so intimate with theirs, on this silvery night, as the river slid along beside them like a snake and the moon watched over them, half-eyed and close to sleep.

No one spoke. When they finally parted, they all smiled at one another, then the couple walked on in silence. *Gordon*, one of them thought. *Gordon*, the other silently answered.

IN
MEMORIAM

Walter Bjorkman
Do the Breadfruit Mash, Baby (May 2010)

I had a breadfruit tree in my backyard in Miami. Well, in my new neighbor's yard, but much of it hung over the fence. Used to be my yard, not really, just an empty lot with the fruit trees on it, owned by the guy who sold me my house, gave me free reign of this fruitfulfiefdom, just for caring for it. Then the Trinidadian new neighbors, then the fence, the orange and grapefruit trees bulldozed. The mango and avocado trees hung over that fence too, providing plenty for all, but were not yet in season. The breadfruit tree was new, transplanted in a condition that bore some small fruit, not ready for harvest, what good is it. And that damn fence that now divided me from my past bounty. I seethed inside, as only the Key Lime tree on my side of the fence was bearing now, so I would pour a coupla Cuba Libres and we would sip them alone in our lounge chairs, staring at the new neighbor's yard and our old trees, muttering to ourselves.

Then they invited us over for a night of masi, the fermented mash beverage from the breadfruit, from their yard back in Trinidad. All was forgiven, the memories of the past becoming a vision of the future and future friends.

First published in 52 | 250 – A Year of Flash

Walter Bjorkman
A Common Creation
(May 2011)

CHILD

A dream of eerie, oddly shaped fish dominated my sleep some nights as a child. Afraid and rapt with wonderment, I could not tear myself away, awaken on will as with other frightful ones. I was slowly suffocating, descending deeper into waters that somehow remained just as clear, and although each non-breath seemed to be my last, it went on and on, intensifying in its awful fascination and constriction on my lungs, until some external factor woke me.

YOUNG MAN

I worked the waters of Miami's gritty river for ten years, sometimes in the cramped hold of a millet-filled ship, where the grain for the hungry Haitian poor was piled everywhere. It got into my lungs, it provided slip-relief, like sawdust, from the oily floor. I also worked the gleaming docks of the shimmering Biscayne Bay where Americans came to bathe in the false hope of the Caribbean, hoping for some days of freedom.

Working in the spacious cruise ship laboratories with their white surgeon's suits and fresh paint, I couldn't help but wonder about the disparities—the Chief Engineer, a man of distinction, the scow captain a man of disrepute.

Then the pure joy of stopping by a Mami-Papi comedor, soaking in fresh-fried maduros where this conflict of Miami faded away into nothingness.

OLD MAN
Now I think of neither but see an azure sky casting diamonds on red coral specks in the sands, and dream of the white foam of a wave receding from your breast.

AFTERWORD

Matt Potter
A Lot (2023)

Berlin, northern summer 2009.

I join a writing group.

But the writing group, convened by a sweet US-expat long in Berlin, is a confusing, long-winded bust.

But I do meet a number of other writers in the group.

Cut to 2010. I am back in Berlin, over the northern summer again.

New writer friends are attending a new writing group, one they hold greater hope for.

And this group is much better—completing writing exercises that are useful and fun and we leave each session knowing we have learned something and developed and had a good time.

At session #2, I am introduced to flash fiction.

We write a very short story in a very short time. My pen flies across the page.

And through the group, I am introduced to *52/250 – A Year of Flash*. I submit a slightly rewritten version of the flash fiction I wrote in session #2, and it is accepted, for Week #9 of *52/250*.

My first online publication. New stories of mine are accepted and published at *52/250*, for the next forty-three weeks.

And I submit to other fiction websites.

But the (un)approachability of some of those websites annoys me.

The idea of starting my own website forms …

Cut to May 2023.

Pure Slush Books publishes this volume you're now holding. It's the 116th book I've published across three imprints.

That's a lot of writers and a lot of words.

Thank you.

Matt Potter
Adelaide, Australia

CONTRIBUTORS

Alex Reece Abbott is a New Zealand-Irish writer published in *Best Small Fictions, Bonsai: Best Small Stories from Aotearoa New Zealand*, and *Heron* (Katherine Mansfield Society), among others. A *Penguin Random House WriteNow* finalist, often shortlisted, she has also won the Irish Novel Fair, Northern Crime, Arvon and HG Wells prizes.
Twitter @AlexReeceAbbott

Tina Barry is the author of *Beautiful Raft* and *Mall Flower*. Her writing appears in numerous publications, including *Best Small Fictions 2020* (spotlighted story) and 2016, *Nasty Women Poets, A Constellation of Kisses*, and *Rattle*. Tina is a teaching artist at The Poetry Barn and Writers.com.

Chelsea Biondolillo is the author of *The Skinned Bird* and two prose chapbooks, *Ologies* and *#Lovesong*. She lives outside Portland, Oregon.

Walter Bjorkman was a writer, poet and photographer from Brooklyn, NY who resided in the mountains of Pennsylvania. His poems and short stories appeared in online journals and in print anthologies. His collection of short stories, *Elsie's World*, was published in 2011. He was Associate Editor of *THRUSH Poetry Journal* and Managing Editor of A-Minor Press. Walter passed away in 2015 and is still part of this community.

Martin Brick grew up in rural Wisconsin. For some weird reason he thought a degree in Fine Art would be a good idea. He earned a Ph.D. in British Lit at Marquette University and currently is an Associate Professor of English at Ohio Dominican University, teaching literature to the next generation of Barnes and Noble slaves.

Diane Brown is a novelist, memoirist, and poet who runs Creative Writing Dunedin, teaching fiction, memoir, and poetry. She specialises in writing long narrative poetic works. Her eight books include the poetic memoir, *Taking My Mother To The Opera* (2015) and the long poetic narrative, *Every Now and Then I Have Another Child* (2020).

John Wentworth Chapin looks back fondly at the 52|250 project as a tremendous spurt of community building and learning as a writer. He lives in Baltimore, Maryland, USA.

James Claffey is an Irish writer and the author of the short fiction collection, *Blood a Cold Blue* (Press 53), and the novel, *The Heart Crossways* (Thrice Publishing). His work has been published in several Norton anthologies and he has been nominated for a Pushcart Prize.

Sheldon Lee Compton is the author of eight books of fiction and poetry. His most recent publications are the short story collection *Sway* and the poetry collection *Runaways*. His first nonfiction book is *The Orchard Is Full of Sound* (West Virginia University Press 2022). He lives in Pike County, Kentucky.

Bob Eckstein is a bestseller, illustrator, *New Yorker* cartoonist, and world's leading snowman expert. He has been speaking publicly against online shopping to raise awareness for independent bookstores and teaches writing at NYU.
Twitter @BobEckstein
Instagram at bobeckstein

David Eggleton's book *The Conch Trumpet* won the 2016 Ockham New Zealand Book Award for Poetry. In 2016, he received the Prime Minister's Award for Literary Achievement in Poetry. His latest book, *The Wilder Years: Selected Poems*, was published by Otago University Press in 2021. He was the Aotearoa New Zealand Poet Laureate for 2019 – 2022.

KM Elkes is the author of flash collection *All That Is Between Us* (Ad Hoc Fiction, 2019). His flash stories have been widely published and won competitions including Bath Flash Fiction Award, Reflex Prize, and the Fish Publishing Prize. He featured in *Best Microfiction 2020*. He's also an award-winning short story author.

Lola Elvy writes music, poetry, and other forms of creative fiction and nonfiction. She founded and edits the online children's and young adults' journal *fingers comma toes*, which hosts the National Flash Fiction Day youth competition. Her work has been featured in online publications and print anthologies.

Michelle Elvy edits at *Flash Frontier* and *Best Small Fictions*, and founded National Flash Fiction Day NZ. Her anthology projects include, most recently, *A Kind of Shelter Whakaruru-taha* and *Breach of All Size: Small stories on Ulysses, love and Venice*. Her books include *the everrumble* (2019) and *the other side of better* (2021).
michelleelvy.com

Nod Ghosh graduated from the Hagley Writers' Institute, Christchurch, New Zealand. Truth Serum Press has published the following novellas-in-flash: *The Crazed Wind* (2018), *Filthy Sucre* (2020), *Toy Train* (2021). Nod has judged the Bath Flash Fiction Award, read for *SmokeLong Quarterly* and *UK National Flash Fiction Day*.
nodghosh.com

Kelly Grotke lives in Essex, Massachusetts, where she feels pretty much at home, most of the time.

Jane Hammons taught writing at UC Berkeley for thirty years. She recently moved back to her home state of New Mexico. Her writing has appeared in *Alaska Quarterly Review, Contrary Magazine, Southwestern American Literature*, and *Tupelo Quarterly*. She is a citizen of the Cherokee Nation of Oklahoma.

Stephen Hastings-King lives by a salt marsh in Essex, Massachusetts, where he makes constraints, works with prepared piano, and writes entertainments of various kinds.

Mary-Jane Holmes is studying for a PhD in poetry and translation at Newcastle University, UK. She has published several collections of short stories and poetry, *Heliotrope with Matches and Magnifying Glass* (Pindrop Press), *Dihedral* (Live Canon Press), *Don't Tell the Bees* (AdHoc Fiction), and *Set a Crow to Catch a Crow* (V.Press).

Randal Houle's poetry and flash has appeared in *Bending Genres, Phoenix, Salmon Creek Journal,* and *52/250 – A Year in Flash.* He is at work on a novel in Washington state.

Gail Ingram writes from the Port Hills of Ōtautahi / Christchurch and is author of *Contents Under Pressure* (Pūkeko Publications 2019). Her poetry and fiction have appeared in journals and anthologies in New Zealand, Australia, UK, and US. She is managing editor for NZ Poetry Society magazine *a fine line* and a short fiction editor for *Flash Frontier.*
theseventhletter.nz

Abha Iyengar is an award-winning, internationally published poet, author, editor. She is a British Council-certified creative writing mentor and founder of Creative Wings Studio. She has authored eight books and edited three anthologies. Her most recent flash fiction collection is titled *The Full Platter* (Hawakal Publishers, 2021).
abhaiyengar.com

Lynn Jenner is a writer and teacher who lives in Aotearoa New Zealand, in the province of Northland. *Dear Sweet Harry*, the account of her obsession with Harry Houdini, was her first book. Lynn has published two other books, *Lost and Gone Away* (Auckland University Press 2015) and *Peat* (Otago University Press 2019).

Erik Kennedy is the author of the poetry books *There's No Place Like the Internet in Springtime* (2018) and *Another Beautiful Day Indoors* (2022), both with Te Herenga Waka University Press, and he co-edited *No Other Place to Stand*, an anthology of Aotearoa climate change poetry (Auckland University Press, 2022).

Jen Knox is an award-winning author and speaker. She is the founder and co-owner of Unleash Creatives, a holistic arts organization located in the US Midwest. Jen's collections include *Resolutions: A Family in Stories* (AUX Media) and *The Glass City* (Press Americana Award Winner).
jenknox.com

Len Kuntz is a writer from Washington State and the author of five books, most recently the personal essay collection, *This is Me, Being Brave*, from Everytime Press.
lenkuntz.blogspot.com

Nathan Alling Long's work appears on NPR and in publications such as *Story Quarterly, Witness, The Sun,* and *Best Microfiction 2020. The Origin of Doubt*, a 50-story collection, was a 2019 Lambda finalist. Other awards include a Truman Capote Literary Fellowship, a Mellon Foundation grant, and four Pushcart nominations.

S J Mannion is a proud Irish woman and citizen of Aotearoa New Zealand. When she can she writes; when she can't she reads. In between she ukuleles.

Al McDermid is an educator and free-lance writer/editor living in Tokyo, Japan. He writes non-fiction, fiction, and poetry, and re-writes translations. He thinks writing about himself in the third person is strange, preferring to write in the first-person, even when not writing about himself.
mcdermid.deviantart.com.

Connecticut resident **Michelle McEwen** writes poems and short stories. Her work has been published in *The Caribbean Writer, Naugatuck River Review, MiPOesias,* and in the anthology *The Best New Poets 2007*, among others. She has also won a short story prize (echapbook.com) for a collection of short stories.

Catherine McNamara grew up in Sydney, ran away to Paris, and ended up in West Africa co-running a bar. *Love Stories for Hectic People* won Best Short Story Collection in the Saboteur Awards (UK). *The Cartography of Others* was finalist in the People's Book Prize (UK). Catherine lives in Italy.

Anna Nazarova-Evans won Ink Tears Flash Fiction competition 2017 and TSS Short Story competition 2015. Her work has also been published by the UK National Flash Fiction Day anthologies, *Word Factory*, *Flash Frontier*, *Spelk*, *Café Aphra*, *Reflex Fiction*, and others. Anna spends most of her days marvelling at the human psyche.
Twitter @AnitchkaNE

Piet Nieuwland's poetry and flash appears in Aotearoa New Zealand and internationally in numerous print and online journals. He is a performance poet and visual artist, and he co-edits the annual Northland anthology, *Fast Fibres Poetry*. A book of his poems, *As light into water*, was published by Cyberwit in 2021.
pietnieuwland.com

James Norcliffe is a New Zealand poet, novelist, editor, and educator. He has published ten collections of poetry, most recently *Deadpan* (Otago University Press, 2019) and over a dozen fantasy novels for young people. His latest book, a novel for adults, is *The Frog Prince* (Penguin Random House 2022).

Tom O'Brien's novella-in-flash *Straw Gods* was published by Reflex Press, and his novelette-in-flash, *Homemade Weather*, was published by Retreat West. He's the winner of the 2021 NFFD NZ Micro Madness and the 2021 Biffy50 Microfiction. His work has been Pushcart and *Best Microfiction* nominated.
tomobrien.co.uk
Twitter @tomwrote

Nuala O'Connor's fifth novel *NORA*, about Nora Barnacle and James Joyce, was a Top 10 historical novel in the *New York Times* and is the One Dublin One Book choice for 2022. Nuala has curated the current exhibition at MoLI—*Love, Says Bloom*. She is editor at flash fiction e-journal *Splonk*.
nualaoconnor.com
Twitter @NualaNiC
Instagram @nuala_oconnor

Michael Parker's poems and flash fiction have appeared in *52/250*, *PoetsArtists*, *MiPOesias*, *Moss Trill*, *Blue Fifth Review*, *Ygdrasil*, *Dialogue: A Journal of Mormon Thought*, and *New Letters Literary Magazine*. He's also the poet of the award-winning collection *Divining the Spirits in the House of the Hush and Hush*.

Gary Percesepe is Associate Editor at *New World Writing* (formerly *Mississippi Review*). His recent books include *Moratorium: Collected Stories 1995-2020*, *The Winter of J* (poems), and *Light Turnout* (poems and stories). He resides in White Plains, New York, and teaches philosophy at Fordham University in the Bronx.

Stella Pierides is a British poet and writer with Greek roots. Two of her books, *The Garden of Absence* and *Of This World*, received Haiku Society of America's Merit Book Awards. She serves on The Haiku Foundation's board of directors and introduces haiku to people affected by Parkinson's Disease.
stellapierides.com

Meg Pokrass is the author of seven flash fiction collections and two novellas–in–flash. Her work has been widely internationally anthologized. She is the Founder and Series Co-Editor of *Best Microfiction*.

Darryl Price has published dozens of limited–edition chapbooks, and his poems have appeared in many journals. He is the author of *The Ferocious Silence* and *The Tiger Who Jumped Over the Moon*.

Sam Rasnake has published work in *Wigleaf, Southern Poetry Anthology, Poets Artists*, and *Bending Genres Anthology 2018 / 2019*, and has served as a judge for the Dorothy Sargent Rosenberg Poetry Prize, University of California, Berkeley. He's the author of *Cinéma Vérité* (A-Minor Press), and *World within the World* (Cyberwit).

John Riley has published poetry and fiction in *Smokelong Quarterly, The Ekphrastic Review, Better Than Starbucks, Banyan Review, Connotation Press, Fiction Daily, The Molotov Cocktail, Dead Mule, St. Anne's Review*, and many other anthologies and journals both online and in print. He has also published over thirty books of nonfiction for young readers.

Robert Scotellaro's work has been included in W.W. Norton's *Flash Fiction International, Best Small Fictions 2016, 2017, 2021*, and *Best Microfiction 2020*. He's the author of seven chapbooks and five flash story collections. He has, with James Thomas, co-edited *New Micro: Exceptionally Short Fiction* (W.W. Norton). robertscotellaro.com

Rachel Smith's prose and poetry has been published in journals and anthologies including *Landfall, Best Small Fictions 2020*, and *Best Microfiction 2019*. She was a recipient of the NZSA Complete MS Manuscript assessment in 2021 and is an editor at *Flash Frontier*.
Twitter @rachelmsmithnz1
rachelmsmithnz.wix.com/rachel-smith

Maggie Sokolik is Director of the College Writing Programs at UC Berkeley, California. She is also Senior Editor at Wayzgoose Press. She plays fiddle, and when the world allows, travels as much as she possibly can. Her first novel, *Too Late for Houston,* will be published soon.

Andrew Stancek clutches onto hope, even in turbulent times. He has been published in *SmokeLong Quarterly*, *FRIGG*, *Hobart*, *Green Mountains Review*, *New World Writing*, *New Flash Fiction Review*, *Jellyfish Review*, and *Peacock Journal*, among others. He has won the Reflex Fiction contest and been nominated for the Pushcart Prize. He continues to be astonished.

T M Upchurch lives and writes in a small house by the sea. Her fiction has been published in print and online, and shortlisted for the Bridport Prize and Bath Flash Fiction Award. She is working on her first novel.
tmupchurch.com
Twitter @tmupchurch

Robert Vaughan is an award-winning author, playwright, and teacher. The latest of his six books is *ASKEW* and his plays have been produced in San Francisco, New York City, and Milwaukee. His work has been widely anthologized, including *New Micro: Exceptionally Short Fiction* and *Best Small Fictions* 2016 and 2019. He is Editor-in-Chief of *Bending Genres*. robert-vaughan.com

Linda Wastila writes from Baltimore, where she professes, mothers, and gives a damn. You can read her work in *The Missouri Review* (2021 Perkins Award), *Epoch Literary Journal*, *Citron Review*, *SmokeLong Quarterly*, *Monkeybicycle*, *Blue Fifth Review*, and *Nanoism*, among others. In between life and writing she grows greens and stuff. linda-leftbrainwrite.blogspot.com

Raised in an Alaskan fishing village, educated at Yale University, **Derek Ivan Webster** is a writer who appreciates a good contrast. When not shepherding students seeking creative careers, Derek pursues his MFA at Fairfield University. It is only his wife, and their precious/precocious co-conspirators, who keep him sane. ivanhope.com/writing
Twitter @ivanhope77.

Iona Winter is the author of three collections: *Gaps in the Light* (2021), *Te Hau Kāika* (2019) and *then the wind came* (2018). She has recently completed her fourth. Widely published and anthologised internationally, her poetry and hybrid fiction have been performed solo and in collaboration with other multimedia artists. Iona is the 2022 recipient of the CLNZ / NZSA Writers' Award.

Cherise Wolas is the author of *The Resurrection of Joan Ashby* and *The Family Tabor*. Her widely acclaimed novels have received literary prize nominations and many wonderful accolades, including *New York Times Book Review* Editor's Choice designations, and have been translated into several foreign languages. She is at work on a new novel.

ACKNOWLEDGMENTS

The editors gratefully acknowledge the editors and presses who first published these works appearing in this collection:

Arvon Foundation
Alex Reece Abbott, 'Antipodean Pepper Tree'

Auckland University Press
Lynn Jenner, 'Pink light' in *Dear Sweet Harry*

Flash Frontier: An Adventure in Short Fiction
Gail Ingram, 'Whispers', and Rachel Smith, 'Night Shadows'

KYSO Flash
Nuala O'Connor, 'Vincent in the Yellow House'

Lakeview, International Journal of Literature and Arts
Catherine McNamara, 'Tales from Bodri Beach'

Landmarks, National Flash Fiction Day Anthology
James Norcliffe, 'Five Travellers in a Small Ford'

Leeds People's Writing Group
Nod Ghosh, 'Coloured Hands'

Lightship Anthology 3
KM Elkes, 'Fair Weather'

Ohio Edit
Erik Kennedy, 'The Personal Responsibility Model of Wildlife Conservation'

Open Pen Magazine
S J Mannion, 'Redemption Song'

Penguin Books New Zealand
David Eggleton, 'Big City Rush Hour' in *South Pacific Sunrise*

Tapas
Abha Iyengar, 'The Price'

The Journal of Compressed Creative Arts
Mary Jane Holmes, 'Set a Crow to Catch a Crow'

Up the Staircase:
James Claffey, 'Bingo Night'

Spelk
Robert Scotellaro, 'Hit Man in Retirement'

Also from Pure Slush Books

pureslush.com/store/

- Marriage Lifespan Vol. 6
  ISBN: 978-1-922427-30-4 (paperback) / 978-1-922427-31-1 (eBook)
- Work Lifespan Vol. 5
  ISBN: 978-1-922427-28-1 (paperback) / 978-1-922427-29-8 (eBook)
- Love Lifespan Vol. 4
  ISBN: 978-1-922427-26-7 (paperback) / 978-1-922427-27-4 (eBook)
- Friendship Lifespan Vol. 3
  ISBN: 978-1-922427-24-3 (paperback) / 978-1-922427-25-0 (eBook)
- Growing Up Lifespan Vol. 2
  ISBN: 978-1-922427-22-9 (paperback) / 978-1-922427-23-6 (eBook)
- Birth Lifespan Vol. 1
  ISBN: 978-1-922427-20-5 (paperback) / 978-1-922427-21-2 (eBook)

Also from Pure Slush Books

pureslush.com/store/

Also from Pure Slush Books

pureslush.com/store/

 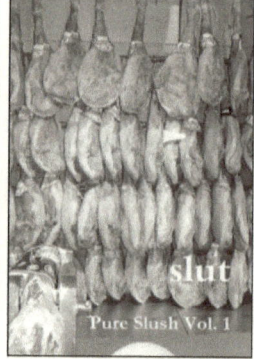 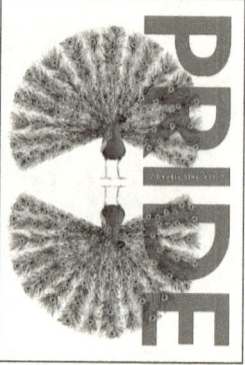

- Five Pure Slush Vol. 10
ISBN: 978-1-925101-71-3 (paperback) / 978-1-925101-72-0 (eBook)
- Feast! Pure Slush Vol. 9
ISBN: 978-1-925101-63-8 (paperback) / 978-1-925101-66-9 (eBook)
- Barcode Pure Slush Vol. 8
ISBN: 978-1-925101-00-3 (paperback) / 978-1-925101-01-0 (eBook)
- Catherine refracted Pure Slush Vol. 7
ISBN: 978-1-925101-78-2 (paperback) / 978-1-925101-79-9 (eBook)
- Slut Pure Slush Vol. 1
ISBN: 978-1-4716-0674-8 (paperback) / 978-1-925101-99-7 (eBook)
- Pride 7 Deadly Sins Vol. 7
ISBN: 978-1-925536-72-0 (paperback) / 978-1-925536-73-7 (eBook)

Also from Pure Slush Books

pureslush.com/store/

- Envy 7 Deadly Sins Vol. 6
ISBN: 978-1-925536-70-6 (paperback) / 978-1-925536-71-3 (eBook)
- Wrath 7 Deadly Sins Vol. 5
ISBN: 978-1-925536-68-3 (paperback) / 978-1-925536-69-0 (eBook)
- Sloth 7 Deadly Sins Vol. 4
ISBN: 978-1-925536-66-9 (paperback) / 978-1-925536-67-6 (eBook)
- Greed 7 Deadly Sins Vol. 3
ISBN: 978-1-925536-64-5 (paperback) / 978-1-925536-65-2 (eBook)
- Gluttony 7 Deadly Sins Vol. 2
ISBN: 978-1-925536-54-6 (paperback) / 978-1-925536-55-3 (eBook)
- Lust 7 Deadly Sins Vol. 1
ISBN: 978-1-925536-47-8 (paperback) / 978-1-925536-48-5 (eBook)